ESSENCE

ESSENCE EXTRACTED BOOK TWO

SURFACED

CAREY DECEVITO

Decevito, Carey
Essence Surfaced / Carey Decevito – Paperback edition
ISBN-13: 978-1-988806-11-2

Cover design by Clarisse Tan, CT Cover Creations
Edited by Karen Hrdlicka

DEDICATION

For those who persevere despite the hurdles against
them…

ACKNOWLEDGMENTS

As always, I'll always owe a great debt of gratitude to my family for their patience and understanding while I hole myself up in my writing cave. Without your never-ending love and support I wouldn't be able to keep up with my writing.

Clarise, my amazing cover designer, words cannot express how your artful gift never ceases to amaze me.

Karen, you are the master of words. Sometimes I wonder how you put up with me and "this" and "that."

Joanne, your keen eye and attention to detail is impeccable. You're never afraid to call me out on a faux-pas. Never stop being you, my friend and coffee date partner.

Kim, you fell in love with this story long before it became a published work. Thank you for being my sounding board, my confidant, my bestie. Love you to the end, girl.

And most importantly, you wonderful readers, bloggers, and fellow authors. Without your support and your push, sometimes I'd think I was doing this alone. Enjoy the continuation to Rafe and Payton's story.

CHAPTER 1

PAYTON

I was matched?

What the hell does that even mean?

And what's more, why had my parents neglected to tell me about our kind having a destined other half?

Were we in so much danger, or was it that rare of a find?

All these questions churned in my head, and I didn't know how to make sense out of any of it at this point. I got up, walked to Rafe's car, and got into the passenger side as soon as he hit the key fob, unlocking the doors. Minutes later, he joined me, turned the key in the ignition, and drove off without saying a word.

I broke the silence first.

"How come I haven't heard of your family until now? I mean, I thought familial friendships usually meant meeting up with one another every once in a while."

His breath signaled his relief as it came out in a whoosh, then he began to explain, "Ours isn't one of the most conventional types of relationships. When threats weren't as popular, our families did get together for fun occasions, but that was before my time—and yours. Then, everything went to shit with the attacks, and my family was forced to move in order to maintain their anonymity. My grandmother was the only one who remained here in Port Hope," he said, glancing over at me then back to the road.

"What are you doing back here then?" I eyed his face as his gaze stayed trained on the road.

"For the same reason I told you before. To help my grandmother out and eventually take over her job as watcher."

"Well, I'd have to say your training is done. Since we've met, you've officially saved my ass more times than I care to count," I mumbled, to which he chuckled.

"A fine ass at that." He winked at me with his signature suggestive smirk, and I couldn't help the heated blush that crept over my entire body, causing me to relive this morning's series of events in my mind.

RAFE

Not knowing what she was thinking about this new reality of hers, I made sure to do up a room for Payton, while she ordered us some Italian food for dinner. I didn't want her to think I expected something out of her. Without saying anything, she seemed to appreciate the gesture.

We spent most of dinnertime in silence, exchanging the occasional glance. I think her mind was slowly formulating questions she would all too soon request answers to; and I was right when she next spoke.

"Can I ask you something?" She stood up and gathered our soiled plates.

"Sure." I followed her to the kitchen in an attempt to help her out.

"I'm hoping you know more about this Fae business than I do, since my parents withheld a lot over the years, telling me it was for my own safety. This is all new to me, with the exception of my empathic abilities, which I've had for some time now."

She sounded so lost and nerve-ridden.

Approaching her from behind, I reached an arm around her waist, my free one aiming to take the plates from her, setting them in the sink. Next, I turned her around so we faced each other. Her eyes looked filled with sadness, and I hoped mine conveyed empathy and understanding as I backed her into the counter's corner.

"There's no need to be nervous," I said on a small smile, tucking a loosened strand of her hair behind her ear.

"How does this whole match thing work, exactly? Is it like werewolves where they bite each other or…" She may have looked contrite about the question, but I got it. She knew next to nothing about our world, and I really didn't mind being the one to fill her in with the knowledge I had.

"Nothing that barbaric in nature," I chuckled. "Because I wasn't born an incubus, I only knew of our matched status once I touched you, when my shoulder blade burned shortly after I made contact with your skin. I checked things out when I got home and found a more detailed symbol etched into my back."

"Ah." She nodded in understanding.

"Our marks are made to evolve when we come in to our abilities. They also change when we discover our destined other half, but only when physical contact has been established between the two," I stressed. "My mark changed to display the symbol of the succubus."

"But how do you know I'm the only succubus you've touched?" she asked. "I know there's no surge of succubi around, but you've been around Carly apparently." She bit her lip. "And she's one. Don't tell me your hands, or anything else, haven't touched in all these years."

"Yeah, but Carly and I aren't matched," I reassured her.

"Okay," she drew out, then bit her lip as if holding

herself back from asking more. It was a lost battle. "So we're matched…and I'm apparently the only one who can alter your mark; what's this whole thing about heirs then?"

"Each Fae family has an heir. You are yours. Carly is her own immediate family's," I explained, but she looked at me suspiciously when I hesitated on the last part about Carly, as if I was leaving something out. She was right. "Being from one of the oldest Fae families, you are one of the most powerful influences out there."

"Like some kind of royal or diplomat?" she asked.

I tilted my head in order to ponder that then decided to nod. I hadn't expected to see her deflate in front of my very eyes. Clearly, she wasn't keen on my response. "If you look at it that way, it's kind of like that, but not quite. There was a royal family at one point, but they've since been eradicated, as far as history tells us." At least was what I'd grown up believing and no one's told me different. "The Fae started with a dozen families. Through the years, these families grew smaller and into extinction, due to hunting, instead of prospering. Only four of the original families remain to this day and we're part of two of them. The other Fae have chosen to either not be a part of the clans and live their lives as humans, no longer practicing their craft or using their abilities; some joined forces with the hunters, or us."

The proverbial choice between good and evil.

"What of these hunters?" she then asked. "These factions, the armies I've been told about?"

I couldn't help giving her a quick squeeze and a sympathetic look. "Your family never told you anything, did they?" I stated aloud more than asking her.

She shook her head, no and answered anyway, "I think they figured I'd be safer not knowing." She let out a huff of evident frustration. "Proves that ignorance isn't necessarily bliss, huh? They did mention I would know when the time was right to stand and fight. Now, I'm not sure if I ever will," she finished on a discouraged note.

"Well, like us, they are part of the ancient families." I paused. "They seek to annihilate those remaining families who aren't willing to side with them. To do so is to kill the host. The one to kill collects the ability, or may capture it with an ancient bottle a witch has spelled to house the soul of the victim, until they decide it is time to give it a new host."

Her body went rigid in my arms. "Okay. Now I'm freaking out a little. Why does it feel like they have a large number of supporters, and we're merely a handful of people?"

I snorted. "Hardly. We're larger than you think," I announced. "And they're not nearly as prepared as we are either. The prophecy is enough to have faith that good will prevail."

Cue the gulp.

"Prophecy?" she asked, her voice squeaking a little.

I nodded. "According to a prophecy, made nearly a hundred years ago, only two families are meant to remain intact in the end. There is no knowledge as to which ones. We can only speculate as to who will prevail in the battle for power; unless you can find an oracle somewhere who'll tell us differently, or who'd be able to let us in on something about the prophecy we haven't come to already know."

I could tell she was beginning to feel overwhelmed by all of this new information I was giving her. When her eyes glazed over, I knew she'd had enough.

PAYTON

Prophecies?

Oracles?

Destinies?

A war?

Magical bottles used for souls?

Was there ever a good time to panic, because right now, I think it would have been justified and well-timed.

"Payton?" Rafe's hand cupped my cheek, bringing me back to the present.

"Huh?" I looked up at his bright blue pools. "I'm sorry. It's so much to take in."

"I know," he whispered, pulling me into his arms, which went a long way to soothe my rattled nerves and give me the courage to ask for more.

"How worried do I have to be?" I pulled away slightly and looked up at him. "I mean, any idea as to when this war, battle, what have you is supposed to happen?"

He actually looked disappointed; not being able to give an answer I'd be happy with as he shook his head, indicating the negative, and said, "I don't know, but something tells me it's going happen much sooner than we would like it."

"So I'm not the only one who feels something big is brewing then?" I asked, only to have Rafe shaking his head once more.

Fuck!

Shivering in disbelief, I broke from his grip and began pacing the kitchen. "I don't think I can handle this," I blurted out. "What about us? Where do we fit in to all of this?" I stopped abruptly, facing him, readying myself for his answer.

"What if I told you that the greatest story ever lived belonged to us?" he proclaimed, with a slight smile forming at the corners of his lips.

"Then I'd say, I might have hit my head much harder than   I   thought   last   night,   and   I'm hearing weird shit," I told him, humor present in my words.

"I speak the truth." He began to close the distance between us and stopped; his face but a few inches away from mine. "I do, however, wish to know what is going on in that beautiful head of yours."

That's when I chose to close the distance between us and deposited a soft kiss to his lips, before nuzzling the side of his nose with mine in appreciation, and whispering, "Thank you." I gave him another chaste peck. "Thanks for explaining some of this to me."

He leaned his forehead to mine. "Welcome."

CHAPTER 2

PAYTON

We spent the evening watching movies and cuddling on the sofa, exchanging looks and the occasional kiss, neither of us pushing to turn our moments into something more heated. Risking an old cliché from your average date night; Rafe walked me to my room, as if it were the end of a date, and kissed me like his life depended on it. It left me weak in the knees, pondering if I should have chased him and worked my own method of persuasion to get him to stay a while.

What is this man doing to me?

Later in the night, I lay in my bed, the sheets down by my waist and my head reeling with thoughts; mostly those of how much I wished to be in Rafe's arms right then. The nightly breeze was coming through the curtains, flooding my room with moonlight, but none of it soothed the yearning I felt, nor relaxed me. The night felt haunting. Eerie.

I rolled over onto my side, my back to the bedroom door as I stared out the window, hoping the breeze and full moon would lull me into a peaceful night's sleep.

I heard a faint clicking sound as the knob to my bedroom door turned. I didn't need the slow dip in my mattress beside me, or his arms wrapping around my waist—

pulling me into his body—or his scent, to tell me it was Rafe. I sensed him before he had even entered; before the floorboards even emitted their slightest creak out in the hall.

"Can't sleep?" I whispered.

"Mmm." He buried his face in my hair. "Apparently, neither can you."

I rolled onto my back so I could see him. Cupping the side of his face, I smiled then said, "I want to hear more about that epic love story theory of yours."

"Is that so?" He smirked down at me.

I nodded. "Or…" I began, not missing the smirk turning into a sly grin on his handsome face. "You can show me."

"You don't have to tell me twice," he said, playfully rolling over me.

Then he made sure to be thorough with both words and actions; narrating his rendition of his story along with his wonderfully sinful invasion of my body.

Sleep had never come so peacefully in the last year up until tonight.

When morning came, I cringed at the thought of having to leave for my shift at the bistro. I think Rafe felt it as well, because he held me against him just a little tighter.

"If I had the choice, I wouldn't go in, but I need the money," I told him, when he pouted as I left the bed to get ready in the bathroom.

Rafe's sulking continued throughout the week, and I loved the fact I wasn't the only one who dreaded having to leave and be without what I'd dubbed as 'my other half' for the duration of my absence. The best part of each day was when he'd come and pick me up after each of my shifts and took me back to his grandmother's expansive home.

When I'd asked him where she was, seeing as I had yet

to be graced by her presence, he'd told me she had been called upon and had left the country for official Fae business.

Friday eventually came and Rafe was there as always, waiting for me, parked at the curbside. I wasn't expecting his foul mood though.

This is a first.

"What's going on? Why so glum?" I asked as I sat in the passenger seat, then reaching for the belt to buckle up.

"We need to talk," he said, driving off before I'd finished securing myself.

Nothing good ever came from hearing those words—whether from man or woman. My stomach lurched at the thought of our impending conversation.

RAFE

"I've been summoned," I told her, as I let us into my home.

"You can't be leaving!" she screeched, turning around to look at me, a panicked expression on her face.

"I have no choice, Payton," I said softly, taking hold of one of her hands. "I've been given a direct order." *From my father.*

"Haven't you told them you found your match?" she asked.

I hesitated long enough for her to formulate her own hypothesis, and she wasn't wrong about it either; at least not entirely.

"You haven't, have you?" The hurt look in her eyes gutted me, her withdrawal stung too as she pulled her hand from my grasp.

Disappointing her wasn't something I was striving for—but had achieved anyway—what with the daggers she was aiming my way with her eyes.

"It's not what you think!" I pleaded.

"Of course not! It's never what *I* think," she huffed and crossed her arms over her chest.

"It's not that I don't want to tell anyone, Payton," I began.

"Then what is it?"

"It's too risky." With the annoyed growl she emitted, I knew I needed to talk and do it fast. "I've told you the hunters are hell-bent on getting rid of matches. There's a reason for that."

"Heirs?"

"That, and…" I stepped toward Payton, tilting her chin up so I looked directly into her eyes, settling my other hand on her hip. "When Fae couples are matched, there exists this surge of power, a bond if you will. That bond is what makes us stronger than our enemy. Haven't you wondered why both your parents were killed at once?"

"Isn't it more of a reason to stay together though? Be at our most powerful when this war begins?"

This whole Fae business was just too new to her. She didn't fully get our way of life; our choosing of certain ways above others that may seem far more logical. Abilities aside, it was like trying to teach a human about the Fae heritage.

"It also makes us look like sitting ducks by staying here," I stated. "The only way around this is if you come with me, and you've said…"

"Done," she blurted.

My jaw dropped. "What?" I had clearly not expected her answer.

"I said I'll go with you." She smiled, her eyes never once straying from mine.

"But you have work," I stated the obvious, still shocked she'd made the decision without much thought; the independent woman that she was.

"And I have a life worth preserving," she whispered, leaning into me, her mouth stopping but a hair away from mine, "with you."

Her eyes were soft as she bridged the remaining gap between us, wrapping her arms around my shoulders to which I held her tightly in return, the only sentiment crossing my mind at that point.

Home.

PAYTON

Truth be told, I didn't know what it was that told me to just leave everything and follow Rafe. I didn't even fully know how I felt for the guy, other than the fact my decision had felt so simple and easy. It had been my choice and mine alone. It hadn't been forced on me by a change in circumstance, despite what you might think; and not once did I question if Rafe had tried to manipulate my decisions with his abilities. Down to the bottom of my soul, I knew it was the thing to do—I would lose him if I didn't follow—and losing him wasn't an option.

Call it instinct, or a leap of faith, even.

My soul knew it wouldn't survive without him; and independence be damned, I was finally going to trust someone to take care of me if it meant we'd be together.

CHAPTER 3

PAYTON

"You have got to be fucking kidding me!" I whined, as Rafe showed me the task at hand. "And I thought my father was a dictator."

For the past week, Rafe had been running me like a drill sergeant with various physical training exercises. For the first time since we'd met, I was seeing a side of him I was beginning to hate just about as much as I was thankful for it. I knew it was important for me to build physical strength so that if hand-to-hand combat ensued—and it would—I'd be able to handle my own, but this was a bit much.

I cursed his brothers for allowing us access to their gym.

Why couldn't Rafe have been a lawyer, even a garbage man, for crying out loud?

So here I stood in this massive gym, alone with Rafe, who was trying to polish up my martial arts knowledge.

"Let's do it again," he repeated, for what seemed like the hundredth time this morning.

He put me through a fight sequence with him as the attacker, asking me to defend myself from his assault. At this point, I seriously wanted it all to end so I made sure to make it count.

With a low roundhouse kick behind the knees, he landed hard on his back, onto the mats that lined the floor.

Straddling his waist with my feet, I hovered above him with a gloating grin. "I think we're done now," I announced.

Talk about bursting my bubble.

Pulling on my ankles, I flew backward onto my butt, as he then straddled my waist with his knees, putting more than the necessary amount of weight on my wrists as he pinned my arms by my head.

That smug son of a...

"Now this is a rather compromising position." He smirked down at me.

Since he wasn't bearing all of his weight down on my waist, I used my feet on the back of his shoes and pushed my feet, scraping down so his knees were no longer under him, then rolled us over so I was back on top of him.

With a stern look to his surprised one, I conveyed I'd had enough. "We're done now," I stressed, as I sat in the exact pose I had taken him down from, but this time, I twisted my feet under his knees to lock our legs together.

"Take a break," he gave.

"Are you trying to piss me off on purpose?"

I knew he wasn't serious, but I wanted to find out just how far Mr. Bright-Eyes-Ninja-Savant was willing to take this. So I leaned in to nibble his jaw, the scent of his after-shave mixed with physical exertion filling my nose. I loved it. Had it been any other man, it would have been disgusting, but on Rafe, it was intoxicating.

"Not at all. It's just..." I nipped his jaw. "Uh..." Licked the nip. "Hmm..."

"What's that?" I backed away, to peer down at his face, before giving the other side of his jaw the same treatment.

"Okay. I give," he said with an exaggerated tone of disappointment.

I chuckled, released his wrists then got up to walk toward the gym locker rooms. "You're so easy," I teased over my shoulder.

"Only with you!" he called out, shortly thereafter, weights began clanging.

This is something I came to discover he did after every one of our sessions. Maybe it was frustration, or something else. I really didn't care, because the sight of his flexing muscles as he worked them, only filled me with desperate desire for him.

Earlier in the week, I expected to have met Rafe's parents, but there hadn't been any sign of them. Then again, there hadn't been much of an opportunity for me to meet them either. If I wasn't training, Rafe had me reading up on Fae history; and when I wasn't doing either, I was eating, sleeping—or we were busy getting busy—for the lack of a better description. It hadn't been until I asked him about their lack of presence this morning that he divulged they had been away on some kind of business trip.

I was pondering this in the gym shower when I felt his hands sneak around my waist, massaging my abdomen, and slowly gliding down toward my core. My back pressed against his front, the lower part of his anatomy telling me I wasn't getting away from him inflicting his pleasuring wrath.

Leaning my head back onto his shoulder, I allowed his hands to have their way with me, as we let hot water rain down over our bodies.

An hour later, we were home, and in our bedroom, dressing for the day, when Rafe announced his parents had called before he so delightfully interrupted my cleaning constitutional, requesting we meet with them. I was petrified about this venture, but just as much excited.

"And here I thought you were ashamed of me all this

time," I joked. The fact he'd kept our budding relationship a secret from everyone—or so I thought—still stung, even though it was initially for our safety.

"Ashamed?" he asked, approaching me with a look of hunger in his eyes. "Never."

Worry caused me to bite my lower lip. "What if they don't like me?"

"That'll never happen," he tried to convince me. "They were over the moon when I told them about you."

"You did what? You said no one knew about us," I repeated his former words.

My blush must have really shown, because he pressed his lips against mine in a nice slow kiss to soothe my nerves.

"I never broadcasted I'd found my match. The Council may not know, but you bet your ass I told my family about you. Feel better now?" he whispered over my cheek, tracing his fingers along my jaw, then wrapping his hand behind my neck, as I tilted my head up to gaze into his eyes.

"Mmm…Much," I managed.

RAFE

Walking into a large den that doubled between an office and library, I spotted my father already sitting behind his desk—with Mom—on his lap no less.

I also caught Payton looking back and forth between Dad and myself. Yes, even twenty-five years older than me, my father and I looked almost identical. Clearing my throat caused my father and my mother, who was embarrassingly—for me—nuzzling her husband's jaw, to turn toward us.

On a nervous giggle from Payton, I squeezed her grip

in mine; then soothingly rubbed my thumb on the top of her hand lightly in a circular pattern, which gained her attention. Giving her a wink, I pulled us over to my father's desk.

"Rafe! And this must be Payton," my mother said, aiming a sweet smile my woman's way.

She got to her feet, walked over to us, grabbed Payton's hands in hers, and then pulled her into her arms for a hug.

"My goodness, child, you've changed so much over the years. You're gorgeous!" she said, looking back at her husband who nodded in agreement. "Just like her mother was, isn't she, Will?"

Say what?

I could tell Payton was just as confused as I was with the way she looked up at me, our perplexed expressions most likely mimicking each other's.

"W-we've met before?" I asked, only to receive a curt nod from my mother.

"You and Payton were so young—two and three I think—I'm not surprised neither of you are able to remember; though that meeting was more in passing than a real visit," she explained. I felt Payton's hand slide back into mine as Mom's beaming smile was now aimed at me. "I hope my son's been treating you the way I've taught him."

Another giggle from my girl.

My girl.

I liked it!

"Yes. He's been amazing, Mrs.–" she began, but Mom cut her off.

"Spare me the Mrs. bit and call me Sandra." She chuckled. "And this handsome man is Will." She pointed to my father.

"So pleased to see you again, sweetheart. I'm so sorry about your parents," he said, getting up to come around his desk, taking Payton into a strong hug.

There was a lot of love in this family. After a year of being alone, I'm sure the woman beside me appreciated it, but since my family can be a bit over the top, I was even surer she also probably felt put off by it.

PAYTON

Rafe's parents weren't all that different from Rafe himself. There was no doubt he had inherited quite a good mix of his folks' characteristics. As hard as I tried to find the eccentricities he had mentioned, what felt like a lifetime ago now, I found none.

Maybe it had been a way to express their Fae abilities, without coming straight out and saying anything, for fear I'd hold it against them despite my own?

The rest of the day was spent with me getting acquainted with Rafe's family. I was thrilled at how natural it felt to be around them; as if I was one of theirs. Sandra's hugs were honest and warm—like my mother's had been. Will loved his wife and family, which made me feel as though he'd do anything to keep me safe. Just as its owners, as large as the mansion of theirs was, it couldn't have felt warmer, more joyful, or bursting with laughter, but most of all, like home. Not much like my house as of late, which felt cold and unlived in. I learned Will was the owner of an architectural firm, and Sandra was a writer of children's books. As for Rafe, he managed a large family gym with his brothers. All in all, they were the perfect, all-American family—tack on the Fae bit.

"Where are Andy and Pat?" Rafe asked, when he came into the room with a tray of refreshments.

"Who are they?" I wondered aloud.

"My brothers." Rafe looked down at me before taking a seat at my side. This was the first time I'd learned their names.

"They should have been here by now," Sandra announced then groaned before continuing. "Hopefully without their lady friends."

"Now, now, Sandra, there's nothing we can do about those two," Will said, patting her leg lightly in reassurance as they shared a smile.

"They're still up to their same old tricks?" Rafe looked at his mother, who made to cuddle into her husband's side.

"You bet!" We turned to see a blond version of Rafe standing there, surely a few years younger, but aside from the hair color, there was no mistaking who his brother was.

"Patrick!" Rafe exclaimed in a motherly tone, which made me giggle, and Patrick's face scrunched up at the mention of his full name.

"Why you can't be like everyone else and call me Pat is beyond my comprehension," he complained and stopped in his tracks, eyeing me up and down. "And who's this hot little number?"

"Manners!" Will said boisterously.

Holding out his hand to me, he said, "I'm Patrick."

"So I've heard." I took his hand and smiled awkwardly. "I'm Payton."

"My girlfriend." Rafe made sure he threw that in for good measure, and I couldn't help the warm blush flushing through my body as he snuck his arm around my waist, pulling me into his side.

It was odd to hear the word girlfriend, seeing as we hadn't made anything official as of yet. Then again, there wasn't a need to do so. For us, it was just he and I and no reason to justify our being together. No labels. It was what it was and that was that. Everything felt easy—natural.

"That's great! Mom always wanted a daughter," the

other man, who I assumed was Andy, said from the doorway.

A brown-eyed, brown-haired man, who looked more like his mother than the rest of the Nottingham clan, walked up to us, pulled me to my feet, and into his arms for a massive hug.

Putting me back a few steps, he sized me up. "Payton, is it?" I nodded. "I remember you," he said shortly after he released me. "You're the girl from my dreams."

That corny line had me laughing before I looked over at Rafe, who rolled his eyes.

"Are these two for real?" I pointed my index finger and motioned between the two of them.

Rafe nodded with a slight upward curling of his lips, evidently happy his two idiot brothers had no effect over me.

After a few minutes of chatting and getting acquainted with Rafe's brothers, Sandra linked her arm around mine and began escorting me out of the den.

"Let's leave the boys be and go enjoy some fresh air. We have so much to discuss." She gave my arm a loving pat.

"Pay?" Rafe walked up to his mother and me.

"Yeah?" I paused and turned to face him, as he gently grabbed my cheeks and gave me a quick kiss, then pulled away with a smile.

"Don't let my mother pepper you with too many questions." He winked.

"I would never!" Sandra teased and Rafe looked over at her with that typical 'You're lying' expression. "Fine. I would, but can you blame me for wanting to get to know the girl that you…"

"Mom!" Rafe gave her a warning look. I couldn't help the giggle that escaped my lips. Life here definitely was far from boring. "Just be good, Mother."

"Rafe, leave your woman be and get back here. We've

got work to do!" Andy winked at us ladies, making me roll my eyes and Sandra tsk at him.

"Well, I'd say you're a hit with everyone, Payton," she whispered, pulling me toward the French patio doors and taking us out to the garden.

I was relieved at her statement. Approval from the matriarch of a suitor's family was big.

"You all make it so easy." I smiled at her.

It was true. I didn't feel like I had to force anything around them.

* * *

Sandra and I had a wonderful conversation. I had learned a bit more about the Fae world from her. Nothing that pertained too much to this war I've been hearing so much about; but more about the Nottingham family tree, some about their abilities, and a tad on their various Fae duties.

"And this is where I pry, if you don't mind?" she asked, as she leaned forward.

"I'm an open book. Pry away." I laughed at my overt statement.

There was simply something about this woman that made me feel at peace—like she wouldn't judge. She made me feel as if I belonged. She was so much like my own mother and perhaps that was the reason for it.

"As a mother, it's in my nature to worry," she began.

I nodded in understanding. "I can only imagine."

"How have you been since your parents' deaths?" she asked, grabbing hold of both of my hands and giving them a comforting squeeze. "It couldn't have been easy on you, sweetheart."

"It wasn't. It's not. It's been Carly and me and that's it," I said.

I spilled my guts about everything that had gone on in the last year: from Gage, to my small circle of friends, the money troubles, work, the nightmares, and the lack of familial support. Sure, I had Carly, but she had her own battles to contend with. In truth, Carly may have been a few years my senior, but we were very much, still kids thrust into an adult world far sooner than our time. What I didn't get was why Carly had the Nottinghams to fall back on, when I was left with only her; seeing as the rest of our family had disowned us for some feud that had always remained unexplained—one that seemed so petty now, considering the future we were to face—and one I will most likely never really hear an explanation for.

"To be honest, it wasn't until I met Rafe that things began to feel right again," I confessed.

She smiled at my remark. "He does have a way, doesn't he?" she said, searching my face for an answer I softly delivered, moments later.

"That, he does."

"Does he know how you feel about him?"

My eyes snapped up to hers, nerves knotting my stomach.

What the hell do I say to that?

"Relax, Payton." She smiled reassuringly. "Your eyes are saying it all, and I couldn't be more thrilled."

I felt myself relaxing a bit more, but only slightly.

"W-we're matched," I stuttered a little.

Just when I thought her smile couldn't get any larger, it did.

"Rafe told me. I'm so happy to hear at least one of my sons has found his other half." She held a hand over her chest, covering the area where her heart was. Something about the way she said those words made me think this whole killing off matches thing was worse than what I had initially thought.

"Is there more than one match for a Fae?" I asked.

The mood grew somber. I couldn't fathom another Fae

being unable to feel the amazing pull and instant chemistry that radiated between two destined individuals.

She shook her head before continuing. "Sadly, there's only one. There are plenty out there who have found love without finding their match, but it's not the same. The bloodline gets diluted and then the powers eventually fade and cease to exist altogether. The bond between two matched people is the strongest you'll ever encounter," she explained.

"What happens if your match shows up, and you've already settled down with someone else?" came flying out of my mouth.

"Ah," she smirked. "Humans might not accept this as easily as the Fae, but once you get to know more of our people, you'll discover triads and quads aren't at all unusual. In fact, we have a few in the family."

Huh?

Then I began to wonder if Sandra could explain why it was I had felt like my soul wouldn't survive if I had let Rafe leave without me. However, I decided that was a conversation better left for another time, seeing as the mood seemed lighter, and I didn't feel it appropriate to possibly darken it.

CHAPTER 4

RAFE

Payton and I were watching a movie on the living room couch when Andy came in. Out of breath and with anger radiating from every pore, his gaze was trained in blind fury on my woman.

"Who knows you're here?" he demanded.

I sensed her immediate panic as her body went rigid against mine. "What?" she shrieked.

What the hell is this all about?

I stood up to defend her and pushed my brother away by a few paces. "Back off, man!" But he kept coming at us. "What's going on?" I inquired.

Pointing over my shoulder, and eyeing Payton with daggers, he yelled, "Your girl here just had us found out!"

"That's impossible!" I protested. "No one knows she's here. No one except..." And my voice trailed off.

"Carly," Payton finished for me on a whisper.

I gave her a small nod. "Payton, you don't think that Carly would...God! I don't even want to finish that sentence because the thought is so absurd!"

She'd been one with us in protecting Payton. Hell, she'd been doing it on her own—with the help of Payton's parents before their deaths—until recently.

"No!" Payton was quick to say. Her simple word was firm and didn't hold a note of hesitation.

"Then we were followed," I announced, dismissive of any other possibility that might exist, or the argumentative air coming off of my own brother, who would believe we'd done something so deliberate.

It's the only other explanation.

PAYTON

"You couldn't just leave her there, could you?" Andy exploded.

I had never seen Rafe mad, but in that moment, I knew I'd rather not see him that way again. His face was red with rage; his eyes darkened to a royal navy color, with his normal gold flecks changing into an almost orange-copper color, while his muscles began rippling through his already tight T-shirt. If shifters were among us, and I hadn't gotten the details from him directly, I'd have thought he was about to change into so kind of animal, he looked so feral.

"There was no way I was leaving her," he growled.

Oh boy!

Scary and hot—that's what he was.

"Why not? Your woman here might have just signed our death sentence," Andy hollered.

"You know damn well–" Rafe was cut off before he could finish.

"What the hell is going on in here?" Will came in, interrupting the argument.

Holy shit!

The Nottingham men were truly alpha in that moment. The air had grown so thick, I had a hard time breathing. Burying myself into the corner of the couch, I folded my knees to my chest and hugged them tight, withdrawing into myself.

How could this be happening?

I couldn't help the tears that began to slide down my cheeks as I rocked myself back and forth, entering some kind of state of delirium.

"You two will calm yourselves down this instant, and talk about this like grown men," their father ordered.

Patrick entered the room behind Will, just as his words had barely left his mouth. The thickening tension began to melt away, and I couldn't help the guilt that seeped through me, running down to the center of my core. I couldn't bear it if something happened to this beautiful family.

That's when I made the decision to get out of there and as far away from all of them as possible. Maybe Andy was right in what he said; I was to blame for bringing trouble to this once peaceful household.

With a heavy heart, I jumped to my feet then ran out of the room, Rafe calling after me; but I was too quick for him to catch up to me.

Grabbing his car keys, which sat on the table by the front door, I darted out of the house.

I made it as far as getting inside the car before anyone caught up to me. I hadn't the heart to put the keys in the ignition, let alone start the damn vehicle. I let my head fall down to the steering wheel as tears poured out of me in frustration, sadness, but most of all, guilt. Someone stood by the driver's side door, attempting to open it. They gave up when they realized I had locked it behind me.

"Payton."

I looked up, baffled at the mention of my name. It wasn't the voice I had expected.

"Gage? What are you doing here?" I asked, confused now more than ever.

"Let me in," he said, holding my teary gaze through the

driver's side window, with a sympathetic one of his own.

Nodding, I did what he asked. Climbing over the gearshift and into the passenger seat, I unlocked the door and allowed him entrance.

Let it be known that I took notice Rafe had yet to make his way outside.

Good. It's for the best, I tried to convince myself.

Gage drove us to a park. I never once questioned how he knew his way around town so well, considering we weren't in Port Hope any longer. I was too distraught to think straight at that point. Instead, I remained submersed in my own thoughts.

Sitting on a swing with Gage on the one next to mine, I tried to figure things out—my head spinning—unsuccessfully gleaning any sense of resolve.

We hadn't said much to each other since leaving the Nottingham residence. Truth be told, I felt bad leaving with Rafe's car and not letting him know where I was headed. After all, he had been tasked to look after me, no matter what kind of predicament I had rained down on him and his family. I sat there for another few minutes, pondering what I should say or do next, wondering about this latest turn of events, which then led to me becoming increasingly aware of the niggling feeling I shouldn't be there.

First of all, how did Gage know where I had been? Secondly, why was he there? Thirdly, what did he want? Feelings of dread filled me when I realized he hadn't even bothered to answer my earlier questions. I slowly got up and turned to head back for the car, thankful Gage had handed the car keys back to me earlier.

I'll leave him here…make a quick getaway.

Had Gage been my stalker—err…follower—this whole time? Why else would he be here and not in Port Hope where I last left him? Hell, we were two and a half hours away from our hometown. Nothing about him being where I was made sense, and that set off far too many alarms in the back of my mind.

This is all wrong.

It was then I felt a strong arm wrap itself around my waist, and before I could scream, his other hand covered my mouth. Fear took over as I scrambled about in my head for a defensive tactic that would work. All I had to do was find a way to get to the car, get in, and drive off, but my trainings—from both my father and Rafe—were evading me in those split seconds.

When my shock wore off, I threw an elbow into Gage's side and heard him groan at the impact, but his grip never wavered.

"If I let go of you, will you hear me out? I don't want to hurt you. I just want for us to talk." I tried to nod against the hand that was covering my mouth, but he hadn't let up enough on his hold. "I'm letting go now," he said.

When his grip released me enough, I turned and pushed him away from me.

"What are you doing here?" I asked, my heart racing.

"I have to talk to you," he repeated, avoiding my eyes.

"We've done all the talking we had to that day on my front porch," I told him. "Kind of a long drive to just have a small talk, don't you think?"

"It's the only thing I could think of," he said.

I really don't like this.

Taking a step back, which he quickly followed up by taking one forward, he counteracted my every move.

"You could have called," I said.

That was a lie. One I knew he was aware of by the skeptical look in his eyes. I wouldn't have answered. Hell, I wouldn't have received the call since I'd blocked every number of his. That final day, when I left him on my door step, I had closed the door on the chapter of my life that included him.

"I had to see you one last time." He closed in slightly on our distance.

This isn't normal.

There was something different in his eyes. It made my skin crawl, so I took another step back, resulting in another one of my paces being matched.

"Why are you really here, Gage?" I asked, and this time, I didn't care who around us could hear. If anything, perhaps it would help me get out of here by drawing attention our way.

"Because I was sent here," he explained. Despite his eyes looking wild, and his demeanor changing suddenly, I knew he spoke the truth; but I couldn't believe my ears. "To take you away," he finished, sounding far too emotionally detached for my liking right then.

"You're a…" My voice faltered when I put two and two together. He seemed surprised that I'd figured him out.

He couldn't be, could he? How could I not have known, though?

"I'm what, Payton?" Amusement shone in his eyes— eyes I no longer recognized. I backed up a few more steps. Steps matched again. "Fae?"

My eyes widened.

He fucking knows about us.

"Yeah. I know about your dirty little secret," he spat, beginning to inch his way toward me once again. "I've known for a while. I know who you are…what you are, Payton."

"Stay back!" I ordered, but he only continued forward, not an ounce of hesitation in his movements.

"Or what?" He smirked. "Your *match* will come and save you? Yeah, I knew of Rafe Nottingham too. By the time he gets down here, sweetie, you'll be long gone."

With a quick pounce, he closed the distance between us.

Adrenaline—my saving grace—kicked in and I found myself screaming out for help, drawing as much attention toward us as I possibly could.

At some point, I could have sworn I heard the screeching of tires in the background. Or was that wishful thinking?

I kicked out into Gage's chest, sending him on his backside. The look of shock on his face was priceless. He quickly got back up to his feet, which I rebutted by grabbing a stick conveniently laid at my feet. I whipped it hard at him, making him move to shield himself from the blow, and thus, giving me the time to shove him back to the ground so I could run away.

"Get the fuck away from me and stay away, or I'll kill you!" I yelled.

His hands wrapped around my ankle and yanked as I tried to run past him—I found myself with my back to the ground, as he snaked his way on top of me, pinning me down with much more force than Rafe had ever used in our training sessions. I tried to push him off of me by bucking my hips, twisting my wrists out from his hands, and that's when the memory of how I got one up on Rafe earlier hit me. Pushing my heels down the back of his legs, I scraped until his knees fell from beneath him.

Please work!

After my third attempt at trying to gain the upper hand had failed, I found myself losing faith in ever being able to defend myself. No one had come to find us. Sure, it was dusk at this point, and the sun was rapidly setting behind the horizon; it explained the lack of population in the park at the moment, but I had expected someone to at least try to intervene.

Suddenly, an idea floated into my head—one I doubted would work.

I have to try.

It had worked to my advantage before. As I feigned weakening, Gage began to relax, smirking with satisfaction at his overpowering me. With his defenses lowered, I pretended to mouth something to him. It was enough to pique his curiosity, because he leaned in like the idiot he was.

You fool!

Capturing his lips with mine, I began to kiss him feverishly, as though my life depended on it. Trying to keep my stomach's contents in check, I felt his hold on me, not to mention, his entire body, weakening. Not being able to take any more of his taste, nor the feel of him on top of me; I pulled away, arched my head back, and brought it forward—hard. That's right, ladies and gentlemen, I headbutted the fucker square on the nose, causing blood to splatter everywhere over my face and the front of my shirt.

Pleased with my blow, agility and speed were my best friends in the moment. I skillfully rolled us over, until I straddled his chest, while his hands were clutching his face. He had to be seeing stars with the force of that blow, because I sure as hell was fighting my own right then.

Shoving myself up and off of him, I backed up, never taking my eyes off Gage's prone and whiny form. It wasn't until I turned to run back to the car that I saw Andy standing there, his eyes wide and mouth agape; then I focused on Rafe who was running toward me.

They'd found me!

RAFE

My feet came to a skidded stop in front of Payton, then proceeded with checking her exposed skin for signs of injury before I took her in my arms, hugging the shit out of her.

"That's the bastard I saw from earlier," Andy announced, walking past me and giving my woman a quick once over with his eyes to ensure she was fine.

"Are you okay?" I asked Payton, halting her efforts to free herself from my grip and making her way toward the car.

"Let me by. I need to get that creep's blood off of me," she huffed, her body shaking with anger; or was it fear? Regardless, I let her go and she turned to head to my car, leaving without an answer to my initial question.

Pissed off, my body shook too, but with definite anger at Gage and at myself. I should have caught up to her much sooner than I had. Hell, she shouldn't have even been able to leave my driveway. Damn my father and brothers holding me back.

I've let her down.

"Payton," I began, as she kept walking toward the parking lot, ignoring me. "Payton!" I demanded.

She dug her heels in the soft grass, turned and gave me an irritated look. "What?"

"Are you okay?" I asked again, following her this time.

"I'm fine."

She didn't have me convinced one bit.

There's no way she could be fine. Hell, I wasn't; and I wouldn't be until all this bullshit was resolved. Something told me I should back off though, so I did. For now.

We were driving back to my parents' house when I finally spoke up.

"Why would you want to leave me?" I asked quietly, the pain of what had transpired a dull dagger to my heart.

I didn't relish having this conversation, especially after what Payton had just been through, but I needed to ease my thoughts and a postmortem of the last few hours had to be had. I wanted answers because I sure as fuck couldn't have her running from me again.

If something had happened to her...

I couldn't even finish that thought.

CHAPTER 5

PAYTON

Plenty of reasons came to mind as to why I had left, but in the silence of Rafe's car, I realized the man sitting next to me had been kept completely in the dark as to the way my mind worked. I had hurt him, of that I had no doubt, but he forgot about my independence as well as the sense of preservation I'd acquired since my parents' demise.

"Why shouldn't I leave? Had I not come along, you'd still all be safe," I explained, my voice cracking with the same guilt that had consumed me earlier and never really dissipated.

"You know that isn't true. All this bullshit would still be happening regardless, Payton. You can't just leave like that."

Okay, so he called me out on my reasoning; kind of like I suspected he would.

I couldn't think of anything to say all of a sudden. Fact of the matter was, I knew he was right. I took a deep breath and forced my gaze to his as we sat at the red light, our eyes locking while he studied my face. Reaching over, he grabbed my hand and brought it to his lap, soothingly rubbing it, sending waves of warmth through and up my arm.

"How did you find me?" I finally asked, as we rounded the corner to his home.

Rafe smiled satisfactorily, parking the car. "You took my ride. I have a tracker on it."

I smirked then sarcastically said, "And here I thought you were just that good."

He chuckled at that. "Funny. Crack all the jokes you want, woman, I would have found you, anytime, anywhere, electronic help or not," he declared, which had me feeling warm and squishy inside. I didn't doubt his capability.

With everything that had gone on today, I was exhausted. All I wanted was to go to bed at this point. Training, meeting the family, and now this whole Gage attacking me thing had taken its toll. The only reason preventing me from giving in to my urges was the adrenaline that was still pumping through me, not to mention the lingering question of why Andy thought Rafe should have left me in Port Hope.

"Why did you think that I told someone about where I was?" I asked Andy, once the three of us had exited our vehicles and reached the front door to the house. Andy had taken a little while longer to reach us because he had decided to track Gage and see where he'd be heading.

"I don't know. I guess it's because I've never seen that guy around before," he announced.

"Where is he now?" I asked.

"I followed him to the other side of town." Andy paused, looked over at his brother, and threw in a single nod as if they knew what the other was thinking. "He stuck out like a sore thumb. Someone seriously needs to teach him how to properly stake out a house."

I had no idea what to say to that statement.

"So you don't even know if he's Fae or not?" Rafe asked, and his brother shook his head, but I could tell there was something more; something they didn't want to talk about with me around.

"But he's in bed with them," Andy said.

Whether Gage was one of us, or not, didn't really matter at this point.

"He's known of us for a while now," I interjected, getting a suspicious look from Rafe's brother. "I didn't tell him. I swear. He told me himself."

His face softened. "I know. I'm sorry for thinking you were behind this," Andy said.

"Well, that's just peachy," Rafe said gruffly.

My face darkened at the memory of those feelings of me being followed. If I hadn't been able to see him while in Port Hope, and Rafe obviously had never seen anything, because I'm sure he would have mentioned something at this point—the watcher, the tracker that he was—then maybe my ex was better than any of us ever suspected. Everything had gone silent and the boys' eyes were trained on me when I looked up.

"What is it?" Rafe asked, turning so he could face me.

Andy looked at me, his arms crossing at his chest. "She's hiding something."

"It's just…it's something I haven't mentioned and didn't think anything of it," I told them. "I honestly didn't know it was relevant until now."

"Just spit it out already!" Andy blurted in an exasperated tone.

"Andrew!" Rafe commanded and noticed the subtle flinch in Andy's posture at the mention of his full name. Rafe turned to face me. "Whatever may seem irrelevant might be the exact opposite, so tell us."

"This has been going on for the past year. It hasn't been constant; up until recently anyway." I paused, attempting to gather the right words. "I've had the feeling I've been followed around for the past month. I never thought it would have been Gage, and frankly, I'm not entirely sure it's just him. He never told me he was the one who followed me around outright."

"Why haven't you told me about this?" Rafe asked. "And no, there were others too, but I've handled them."

Swallowing my surprise at this information, I said, "I did. Well, sort of. That night when I ran into you on the street, running like a mad woman. The night Carly was attacked. And then…"

"Wait! What? Carly was attacked?" Andy blurted out, stopping me mid-sentence when I was recounting the time when Rafe had rescued me from my two intruders. I nodded and looked back at Rafe, noticing a slight hint of worry on Andy's face before doing so.

What's that about?

"Still, you could have said something about the fact that night hadn't been the first time." Rafe paused. "I'm supposed to keep you safe. How can I do that if you're not telling me everything?"

"It wasn't my first time being followed, but it was my first being chased down," I told them calmly then narrowed my eyes on Rafe. "And for your information, you could have said something about those other stalkers long before now."

"What else aren't you telling us?" Andy's eyes were suspicious, but his gaze softened almost immediately when he noticed the look on my face. I could tell he thought I felt helpless in all of this; that I was only doing what I thought was best for everyone all around.

"That's it."

I looked at both of them and then averted my eyes, my gaze aimed at my feet. Sure, I felt guilty about keeping that information from Rafe, but then again, why would I divulge information when I doubted its relevancy? Anyone would have done the same thing I had. Until this whole succubus business began, I chalked it up to an overactive imagination, or perhaps some perverted creep who was keeping tabs on me. So I did like anyone else and made sure my windows and doors remained locked and went about my life.

It wasn't until I had entered the shower in our en suite bathroom that I collapsed to the tile flooring. Giving in to the rush of emotions flooding my senses all at once: the fear, the anger, and the frustration. I felt so alone in that moment. In truth, I knew I wasn't. I knew Rafe would have never let anything happen to me, but…

What if I hadn't been able to fend Gage off? What if Rafe and Andy hadn't managed to track me? I shuddered at the thought.

I sat there, on the cold tile floor, water raining down on me, until the shower stall door opened. The water—now turned cold—stopped running, and strong arms wrapped around me with a towel as I sobbed into Rafe's neck.

Dried off and cuddled into my man, I found myself drifting off to the soft sound of his heart's rhythm. My question, as to why Andy thought I should have been left behind in Port Hope, was partially answered and new questions forming; like what was the tie that bound Andy and Carly? But tomorrow was another day; one where I would discover more answers, hopefully.

CHAPTER 6

PAYTON

As always, it had been a bright and early morning of training at the family gym. I found out, shortly after meeting Rafe's brothers, Patrick was the one who managed the establishment, while Andy was one of their trainers. As much as I still cursed them all for allowing us round-the-clock access to their first-rate facility, part of me was thankful.

Truthfully, I could have used a day off. However, knowing a little more about what I was dealing with, after yesterday's incident with running off and nearly being abducted by Gage, I knew I definitely should concentrate more on training.

Rafe voiced he was impressed with the way I had handled myself, but nonetheless advised my feminine wiles might not always be useful to get me out of a tight situation. There were others out there who wouldn't be fooled by my tactic, or wouldn't be affected by it.

Needless to say, I was taking this morning's training session much more seriously than I had taken all my others. Even Patrick and Andy had joined us—making it a full-fledged family affair, since Rafe's brothers had called him out on going light on me, thus not doing me any favors.

As much as my dedication beckoned my attendance and efforts, my mind wasn't in the game though. It could have been due to the lack of sleep last night or my not being able to focus long enough.

I missed the girls—Sahara in particular—and I couldn't help but worry about Carly, who was now officially on her own in Port Hope. I hadn't been allowed to call and check in with her regularly, like I'd promised her, on the off chance someone was listening in on our calls or tracing them.

Maybe I could convince my match to let me call Sahara and get her to check up on my aunt.

"Payton, you need to focus!" Rafe stated in an exasperated fashion, after I was sent to the floor mats another dozen times.

Shaking my latest tumble off, I got back up and braced myself. My body still ached from last night.

Just then, the gym doors opened, and four colossally menacing men walked in; looking for what seemed like a score to settle. I knew this couldn't be good. Andy and Patrick came to flank Rafe and me on the mats.

"I suggest you turn around and walk back out to where you came from. You're not welcome here," Patrick growled.

"Relax, Cujo!" the tallest of the four said. "We're simply conveying a message."

"And...what is it?" Rafe crossed his arms over his chest, stepping slightly forward, so I was now behind him as Andy pulled me back. He and Patrick stood in front of me, forming a wall of muscle.

What was that for?

"You better watch her," that same tall goon told us, nodding toward me. "She'll be with us before you know it."

Rafe's fists balled tightly at his announcement, making

the other three chuckle. Andy and Patrick growled. All three of my men were rigid with fury.

"She's mine," Rafe then growled.

"I heard she'd found her match. Is that right, puppet?" He glanced over at me then back to Rafe. "I'd beg to differ."

I didn't say or do anything that would give him the answer he was searching for, but I knew he didn't need confirmation. Word traveled fast, and I was sure Gage was somehow attached to this morning's events.

"You know, I can satisfy you more than he can." He freakishly wagged his disgusting tongue at me, as I quickly averted my eyes from the scene, chills running down my spine and nausea washing over me.

"I suggest the four of you run along," I venomously spat, my gaze sternly trained on them, then focused on the largest of the four—the one claiming I'd be his—the leader. "I'm not yours, nor will I ever be. I would rather die than go freely with you."

"That can be arranged, but what a loss it would be," the lead guy said, licking his lips as he eyed me from head to toe. "Come on, boys." He turned to leave, the other three standing there, sizing me up as he had, smirks prominently displayed on each one of their faces. "I'll get a piece of that sweet ass soon enough, and then it'll all be over."

Once he was done, the other three followed.

When they disappeared from where they came, the leader, having waited for the men to clear the door before he made his exit, turned around to face us one last time.

"The name's Matt. I suggest you remember it, because that's the name you'll be screaming out when I fuck you senseless and make you mine." He laughed out loud, the sound reverberating over the gym's concrete walls. "Watch your backs."

"It'll never happen," I hollered, despite him having

disappeared. "If it's a war you want, it's one you'll lose, you bastard!"

I wanted to wipe the smug look of confidence right off of that Matt character's face. I didn't even realize Andy and Patrick were both holding me back by my arms until I felt the pinching of skin.

Who the hell does he think he is?

"I think we can call this a day." Rafe turned to look at me when the coast was clear. I shook my arms out of his brothers' respective holds. "We need to get you back home."

Did I miss something?

"But we're not done," I told him.

In actuality, I was tired and couldn't wait until we were done, but I found myself filled with rage—thanks to those four Neanderthals—so I was sort of hoping I could blow off some steam.

"This isn't the time to put up a fuss, Payton," Andy warned.

Rafe walked up to me and attempted a reassuring smile, which failed miserably.

"Other than the obvious pending war, the quadruplets of doom and gloom, and last night, what's wrong?" I asked him in particular.

He took my hand and pulled me toward the exit.

"I'll tell you on the way home," he said softly.

Looking back behind me, Andy nodded in our direction as Patrick nudged him and began walking toward the exit too.

"We'll be right behind you," Patrick called.

RAFE

We were halfway to my parents' house, and not a word had been uttered with the explanation I knew Payton was seeking. To be honest, I was trying to find a way to put things so she wouldn't freak out, because I could tell from her fidgeting she was already wired for sound.

"So are you going to tell me what this whole sudden panic and need to get out of here has come from, or do I have to beat it out of you and your brothers?" she asked, with her arms crossed over her chest.

After a long drawn out breath, I asked, "What do you want to know?"

"First of all, who the hell were they?" she said then continued, "And secondly, why are they so adamant to have me, other than to satiate Matt's sexual needs?" Disdain dropped from her every word, and the shiver of disgust didn't assuage the building rage inside of me. I could have killed the fucker, but I couldn't do it. Not yet anyway. We needed more information before that could happen.

Growling out some of my frustration, I proceeded to explain. "Matt Davis is not just any regular goon, Payton. He'll definitely try and get you for himself: for their side. The other three are his buddies; his bodyguards, I suppose."

Her eyes were glued to the side of my face. "You're talking like I'm the key to this whole thing."

You don't even know the half of it, sweetheart.

With my jaw clenched, instead of saying what I was thinking—what I'd learned earlier today—I led with, "I think you're better off speaking to my parents about all of this."

"Why? I'm asking you," she said, clearly irritated from my dodging her question. "You told me before you'd answer all of my questions, so are you telling me you lied?"

Bringing the car to a full stop and positioning the shifter to the 'P' position, I turned to face her, our eyes connecting and then said, "Yes, you are the key to all of this."

The shock I expected, but the concern and fear sparkling in her eyes had me reaching over the middle console to grab her hands in mine.

All right, confession time.

"There's more about you that you don't know," I began.

"Tell me, Rafe," she pleaded, biting her bottom lip. "Wouldn't I be better prepared if I knew?"

"Yes and no," I sighed. "The more people who know or suspect it, the worse off we are. I can't take the chance of losing you." The emotion in her eyes was overwhelming. "I don't think I'd be able to live if we couldn't be together."

"Why would you lose me? No one is taking me away." She was so matter-of-fact. "I'm glad I'm not the only one who feels this way then."

"What do you mean?" I asked, one of my hands moving to cradle her cheek.

"When you told me you were leaving…" I nodded that I understood what she was referring to. "I felt like I would die if I wasn't able to be with you." I found myself grinning at her revelation. "I can't be without you, yet I don't understand why that is, but I need you, Rafe."

A knock on the passenger side window made us jump, then the door opened, thus ending our sweet moment. Andy waited for Payton to get out, as Patrick followed us into the house with me in the lead, pulling my woman along by her hand.

"Go get yourselves cleaned up, and I'll make sure to let Mom and Dad know that we need a family meeting," Andy announced.

PAYTON

I felt manhandled.

Rafe had pulled me into our shared bedroom and shut the door quickly behind us.

"About just now," I said, looking at Rafe who stood before me, conflict lacing his eyes. "What was that?"

"What?" He feigned innocence but couldn't hide his smirk.

"That thing…" I started, but he quickly closed the gap between us with his lips; giving me the most slow and sensual kiss that made my mind turn to mush. My knees wanted to buckle.

Smirking as he pulled away, he said, "You were saying?"

"I-I…" I said breathlessly, as I attempted to close the space between us, but after our lips touched, he pulled away, making me crave more of him instantly.

"We need to meet up with my parents," he reminded.

"I know." I gave him my best pout and he chuckled. "And don't think I haven't forgotten that you refused to answer me."

Cradling my face in his hands, he said, "I needed a moment with you." He pecked the side of my mouth. "Have dinner with me tonight. Just me and you."

"Just us?" I asked, and he nodded in response.

"I need some alone time with you," he said, kissing the tip of my nose, making me scrunch it up because his lips tickled.

Excited at spending time alone outside of the bedroom, my mind conjured up possibilities of what he could have planned for us.

CHAPTER 7

PAYTON

A little over half an hour later, I headed downstairs by myself. Rafe had disappeared from our room in the short time I had been in the shower. I figured I'd join him and the others in the den, which seemed to me as being the usual family meeting spot. As I entered the room, all were there, and everything grew increasingly quiet while everyone turned to look at me.

"Do I have something on my face?" I asked, reaching up and feeling self-conscious all of a sudden.

"You're absolutely beautiful, sweetheart," Sandra said.

Rafe smiled at me as he extended his hand for me to take. "Gorgeous," he added.

"We have a few things to discuss, I understand?" Will looked over at Rafe and me.

"The Davis clan is onto us more than we initially thought," Rafe told his father. "They want Payton for themselves."

"I figured this would happen, sooner than later," he said, and turned to me—noticing the look of disgust on my face—judging by the chuckle he let loose. "I see he's made an impression on you."

I nodded and huffed, "He's a pompous jerk who thinks he's about to get what he wants. I hate people like that."

Sharing every detail of what had transpired earlier this morning at the gym, Will advised that I go nowhere without all three of the boys.

"You need to stick with her no matter where she goes, you hear me, boys?" he said. "I'm making it known that the Davises know of her status."

My status?

Evidently I must have spoken my thought aloud, because Will turned to me with a sympathetic eye. "It's simply for the time being, sweetheart; or at least until we know more about what they're up to."

As the family meeting let out, Will set out to call his contacts and notify them of what had been going on, while Rafe, his brothers, and I started out of the room.

"Payton, sweetie? Will and I would like to speak with you once he's off the phone," Sandra announced.

Rafe turned to me. "Did you want me to stay?"

"It's okay," I told him. "I'll be fine."

"Actually, Rafe, maybe you should sit down too," Will told him, as he slid his finger on his phone's screen to disconnect the call he was on.

"That's not possible!" I was feeling hot and seeing spots floating about in my field of vision, but I had to keep pacing. It was about the only thing keeping me from punching someone or something right then.

Adopted?

My life flashed before my eyes. My parents, or whom I thought had been mine—weren't really—from a biological standpoint.

I couldn't quite wrap my head around this latest revelation.

"There's more," Will began slowly. "You might want to sit down for this one."

Rafe grabbed my hand, pulling me down beside him, rubbing gentle circles on the top of it with his thumb.

Looking at the man who held me together with a simple soothing touch, I said, "You know what's next, don't you?"

"Some," he told me. "This is why I wasn't as open earlier with your questions. My parents are better suited to give you the answers you're looking for."

I sat through them telling me that the royal bloodlines were thought to have been extinguished altogether—basically the same rendition I had gotten just before we'd come to Rafe's parents' home from the man himself. What no one knew was a coup had been staged a few generations ago, which prevented this total eradication of the royal bloodline. As it stood, I was it—just me, myself, and I— the one and only Royal.

Don't get me started on how I feel about this latest news. If Rafe wasn't at my side, I'm pretty sure I'd have passed right the hell out.

So let me get on with it…

Having gained the help of a witch, a spell had been cast, preventing even the strongest of oracles to see a Royal ever ascending to the throne again. In its stead, they were fed the illusion of two families gaining true power, hence where this prophecy I had been hearing about had been born. What happened to the Devonshire's heir was absolutely heartbreaking. He had been sacrificed in an attack, but due to the similar physical traits, it had been easy to trick everyone. Only one family was in the know of this information—the Nottinghams.

"This is why the balance can be tipped in either

direction, isn't it?" I surmised aloud. "Everything hinges on me…my decision." If I sided with the Nottinghams, then I'd be tipping the scales toward good. If I sided with…

There's no fucking way that's going to happen.

"I'm afraid so," Sandra said, knocking me back to the present. "I need you to come with me, now. There are things only a woman can address with you at this point." I looked at Rafe. "Don't worry, sweetie, Will needs to talk with Rafe also."

She came to me and grabbed my hand, pulling me away. I turned to look at Rafe and couldn't help the smile on my face at the stunned look he had on his. The deer-caught-in-headlights expression on him was a priceless one.

CHAPTER 8

PAYTON

I had been shifty for the rest of the day, avoiding Rafe as much as possible thanks to Sandra. This had definitely been a day to top all days from a news standpoint. Needless to say, I never felt any more insecure about who I was as a person. Everything I was; everything I've done; none of it was ever truly me, now was it? I sat there, on the edge of the bed, remembering the conversation I had with Rafe's mother earlier...

Sitting in the garden as we had the previous day, I couldn't help the nervous energy coursing through me. It only heightened when Sandra finally sat across from me. That's also when I realized I was inadvertently feeling some of her nervousness along with mine.

Damn empathic abilities, can't you ever go off on holiday for once?

I shifted in my seat, waiting for our conversation to start; I had the distinctive feeling this was going to be an awkward one for the record books.

"Sweetie," Sandra began and smiled. "You remember the talk we had yesterday about how you felt for Rafe?" I nodded in comprehension and urged her to keep going. "Uh..." She rubbed her hands, palms down on her thighs.

This was evidently tough for her. "This is a conversation a mother has with her daughter, and because yours isn't able to be here, you'll have to please bear with me on this one."

"Whatever it is, I'm sure it's not as bad as you think," I said, patting the top of her right hand that still lay on her lap.

"It's not bad. It's just…I never thought I'd be having this conversation with my son's girlfriend." She blushed slightly.

"Oh?" I looked at her, my eyes widening in slight comprehension as to where this conversation was headed, her nerves beginning to get the better of me along with herself.

"It's about you being a Royal and your match," she said. "How you become truly matched."

"I know it has something to do with the first touch of the succubus and then there's…" My voice trailed off momentarily as I struggled to get my bearings and over my embarrassment. "Sex," I blurted almost at a whisper.

Imagine my predicament of having to speak about sex, with my boyfriend's mother of all people! It kind of freaked me out. Then again, no one knew more about all of this than she and Will. My supposed parents had, but they weren't there, were they?

It still doesn't make this part of things any less awkward.

"We're not in the nineteenth century, and I know how things go," she began. "I know that you've been together." I felt my heated blush come over me. "But I also know the royal matching isn't complete."

That's when Sandra told me about the Royal bonding process. I couldn't help but wonder if Rafe knew about any of this.

"No. He caught his father and I discussing you, and your being Royal, this morning. He had us explain a bit to him before you all left for the gym. Other than that, he doesn't know anything other than the fact you're of royal descent," she divulged.

"I see," I pondered aloud. "So what you're telling me is, that even though Rafe and I are matched, we haven't completed the *Royal* process?"

She nodded. "You need to complete the series of them on the first full moon after you've happened upon your match," she explained.

"But that's tonight!" I exclaimed.

Another nod. "If not, then all will be lost; from a Royal perspective that is."

Talk about a bomb. The pressure cooker was definitely set to high now!

A knock on my door was what shook me out of the memory of my earlier conversation with Rafe's mother.

"Come in," I croaked.

The door opened and in walked Andy; definitely not the person had I expected to see.

"Just making sure you're okay," he said; his eyes unable to make contact with mine.

"I've been better," I admitted.

"You've got everyone worried about you downstairs," he divulged, this time, his eyes finally meeting mine.

"I know. It's just a lot of information to digest all at once," I told him, and nervously flattened my red strapless dress over my thighs; trying to rid it of its nonexistent wrinkles.

I knew it wouldn't be long until Rafe would come to find me for our date. My fidgeting was getting worse by the minute. The fate of the Fae world having a Royal on a throne again hung in the balance because, in just a few hours, I had to make the biggest decision of my life.

Thanks a lot Mother Nature.

Would I risk it all and be a regular Fae, or give in to

what now was beginning to feel right? Could I bring peace to my kind again, and take on my responsibilities? At this point, I had no clue what they entailed. I knew the Nottinghams were here to help me along the way, and with Rafe by my side, I felt like I could take on the world. So much had to be said and done in the wake of tonight; and it all hinged on me being able to fulfill this dream everyone else had of wanting—no, *needing*—a Royal back to restore balance to all things Fae.

A soft knock came a second time on the bedroom door. My heart felt like it wanted to jump out of my chest, as nerves once again began to get the better of me. Andy opened the door to reveal a handsomely dressed Rafe, in a white button-down shirt, rolled at his elbows, and black dress pants; the top buttons of his shirt left undone to reveal the beginning of his chest. One word came to mind…

Sexy.

He literally took my breath away.

Before leaving us, Andy turned and looked me over in an almost adoring way. "We'll be leaving now. You look beautiful, Payton" he finished on a blush.

Despite his initial shortcomings, Andy was a good man. Sandra might not see it as clearly as I do with Andy and Patrick, but they were both good guys. She raised them right. Urges aside, their hearts were in the right place when it mattered most.

RAFE

Our eyes were fused together, but I was hesitant to go to her. "Hi," I said, the physical pull too great between us to ignore at this point.

I hadn't seen Payton since this morning in the den.

Despite my nerves, which had magically disappeared somehow, and the hodgepodge of thoughts rolling around in my head at the moment, my feet made their way to her. Letting go of the breath she'd been holding onto, I wrapped my arms around her and kissed her forehead. I took notice of her scent mixing with a rather light floral perfume I didn't recognize.

Pulling away slowly, Payton gave me a sweet smile, then muttered a shaky, "Hi."

"Ready?" I asked.

Once she nodded, I took her hand and pulled her along with me down the stairs.

Steering her toward the back garden, her gasp of surprise made me feel lighter and relieved that she appreciated the effort I'd made for our true first solo date.

There, in the middle of the mix of hydrangeas, rose bushes, and other beautiful flowers, their names evading me at the moment, was an elegantly decorated table and two chairs. Coupled with the setting sun, everything looked like it was taken out of Mom's favorite romance novels, which she'd occasionally indulge in.

Pulling Payton to one of the chairs, I helped her sit down. Her girly giggle was one of my favorite sounds in the world, or so I'd come to realize while spending so much time with her over the last few weeks.

"You did this?" she asked, her eyes holding mine from across the table.

"I had help," I confessed, my voice unwavering as I reached for, and then poured us some champagne.

After I handed her one of the flutes, I held mine up in a gesture for a toast.

"I don't do toasts," I said quickly, as I felt a slight flush spreading onto my face before I continued. "Mainly because I never know what to say."

"How about…" she paused to ponder what to say next, "…to living in the moment?"

I laughed lightly as we clinked glasses and repeated, "To living in the moment."

PAYTON

Dinner was great. Rafe had ordered us pizza. Yeah, I know, pizza! It was odd for the setting, but he'd indulged me with my favorite food. So here we were, sipping expensive champagne and eating pizza in comfortable silence as we stole glances from one another.

"How was your chat with Mom?" he eventually asked.

My face burned, and judging by the grin on his face, I knew he enjoyed my reaction. I was just thankful I had no food or drink in my mouth to choke on or spit out when he'd asked. Talk about mortifying!

"You know about it, I'm sure your mother filled you in on some," I said.

"I knew it was the reason you've been avoiding me all day," he said quietly.

"I'm sorry," I began. "It's just so much to digest."

"Anything I can help you with?" he asked.

"You can answer one question for me."

"Anything," was his response.

"How come you're not every bit as freaked out as I am?" I asked.

Instead of answering me right then and there, he got up and came to kneel beside me, our faces mere inches in distance from the other.

"There's something I haven't told you," he said, tucking a loose strand of my hair back behind my ear, our eyes exchanging a variety of emotions. "I love you. I think I always have and I always will. Even before I met you, I loved you. I don't care what we do, I know it'll be great so long as we're together."

My heart raced, and my body took over for me as I grabbed his face in my hands and crashed my lips to his, forgetting about all this talk about royalty-this, and war-that. I simply wanted to do what felt right—natural. I knew I didn't want to lose Rafe. I couldn't. Most importantly, I knew—right then, that is—I had to follow through with this newly acquired destiny of mine. My succubus urges were becoming stronger and stronger—harder to deny they would be, according to Sandra—and I felt myself failing to keep the vixen in check. The horny bitch wanted out, especially while my lips tasted Rafe's.

He managed to pull himself away from me, breathless, darkness consuming his irises with lust. "I didn't expect that kind of a reaction." He smirked, making light of his revelation.

"You can't say that to a woman and not expect her to be all over you." I smiled shyly, as he proceeded to find his seat and I got up.

"Where are you going?" He looked at me confused.

I walked up behind him and kissed his ear then nibbled his lobe, smiling at the groan that rumbled in his throat.

"I'll let you in on a little secret," I whispered. "I love you too."

As I turned to walk back toward the house, our shared room my intended destination, I felt his hand on mine, pulling me back to him as he remained seated on his chair. Forcing me to sit on his lap, I couldn't ignore the part of him that was now standing at attention for me, nor the look of tenderness that filled his eyes where moments ago, only lust reflected.

"You can't say that to a man and just walk away." He mimicked the tone I had used with him before his hand found its way, gently wrapping itself around the nape of my neck, pulling my lips to his.

CHAPTER 9

PAYTON

Phase one of three of our royal binding was complete. I hadn't expected for it to happen, but I realized my proverbial heart wanted what it wanted, and simply stifling my feelings wasn't going to work.

Rafe and I had been so deeply wrapped up in one another; we failed to notice the person who had been standing there until he cleared his throat. Jumping slightly, with Rafe bracing me to keep me from falling off his lap, we both turned to find Will standing with a smile on his face, his eyes twinkling.

"I thought you were all gone," Rafe mumbled.

I was feeling embarrassed but also disappointed at our interruption.

"I was, but I came back to look in on you two." He smirked.

"We're fine," Rafe said, nuzzling the side of my jaw, barely paying any mind to his father.

"I see that," he chuckled. "You two are glowing by the way; get a room!"

He turned and left us with a hearty laugh following him.

"I think that's the best idea I've heard yet," I told Rafe,

as I met his lips with mine, nibbling on his bottom one, making him groan.

He evidently didn't need any more convincing as he whisked me up into a bridal style hold and raced us into the house; forgetting all about the rest of our dinner, which we had only just begun.

He set me on my feet, at the foot of the bed, never once taking his eyes off of mine. He seemed as if he was searching for something in them, and I sensed his worry. I didn't know why my empathic abilities were wreaking havoc on my senses all of a sudden, but I was glad at this moment. It only proved that this solid man in front of me had his own set of worries, just like anyone one else I knew, including myself.

"What's wrong?" I asked softly, my hand reaching up to his face.

"I don't know where your head is at with all of this royal business," he explained.

I did the best thing I knew to do. I kissed him—hard and passionately—slipping my tongue into his parted mouth, eliciting a soulful moan from him before I pulled away to look at his face once more.

"I spent the entire day freaking out about this whole thing," I told him, as I nuzzled his jaw slightly, then pulled back again and took a deep breath. "I want peace, Rafe, and I can't help the motions I need to take to get there. It's like something inside of me is urging me to go through with it. Turns out that what I was making complicated in my mind never could have been more simple."

He cupped the side of my face with a loving hand. "But why do I sense fear?" he asked.

"Don't get me wrong, I'm terrified." I tried to stray my gaze somewhere else, but my eyes wouldn't budge. They were fused to his glowing sapphire pools. "I have no clue what this whole royal destiny will hold for me—for us—but the thought of losing you is too much to bear."

"You'll never lose me," he vowed, and I knew he intended to keep that promise, but I simply couldn't shake the feeling that was building inside; telling me I needed to complete this whole process. No one really knew what fate would hold for us down the road.

I needed his mark on me, I needed all of him, and most of all: I needed to end this age-old pending war in its entirety. I wanted my happily ever after. Yes, I said it! Now, go ahead and call me a sentimental sap, but you'll end up admitting it's exactly what you'd want for yourself too.

"I love you too much to let anything happen to us," he proclaimed, his eyes growing slightly darker, as my fingers played with the hair at the nape of his neck. "I'll follow you to the ends of the world."

"So you're okay with this?" I asked.

"I'm all in, Payton," he whispered against my lips.

His fingers rubbed up my back as he found the zipper to my dress, slowly unzipping while he let their tips lightly graze my skin, sending heated shivers of lust, which caused me to gulp, my breath to hitch, and my eyes to close as I savored the sensation. His lips made contact with mine and trailed down to my jaw, alternating between nibbles, licks, and more kisses until he had reached my neck then collarbone. Arching into him, my body betrayed me as my knees began to weaken. Rafe grabbed hold of my butt and palmed it, pulling me closer to him, my mouth colliding with his in a feverish kiss, our tongues dueling. My feet found the floor and regained stability, as Rafe pushed the remainder of my dress down to my feet, leaving me in my lacy red strapless and barely-there underwear.

"I'm glad you like it." I smirked after he took a long have-mercy-type look at me, a gulp distinguishable.

"You're beautiful," he said breathlessly.

I approached him with the one step I needed to take, as he watched me start unbuttoning his shirt, letting my eyes feast over his body. Bringing my mouth to his chest, I pleasured his heated skin with a few nips and licks while I pushed his shirt off of his shoulders, feeling the muscles of his arms flexing as my fingers gingerly played the length of them until he grabbed my hands, which caused me to look up as he took my mouth.

Craving closeness, Rafe let go of my hands as he pulled my hips toward him. My hands went on another mission as they found his belt buckle, my fingers fumbling about clumsily out of urgency.

He lay over top of me, kissing, eliciting the most wonderful tingles throughout my body; making it throb with need. The sinful things that mouth of his was capable of doing had me begging for the feel of him inside my most intimate of places.

"I'm planning on taking my time with you, tonight," he announced, as he came back up to meet my eyes.

"Rafe," I moaned into his mouth in the midst of our carnal warm-up.

I didn't know how much longer I could take it. I needed him like a plant needs water in the desert. Moments later, I felt his erection at my entrance—no condom this time. An interesting fact had been brought up between Sandra and myself; apparently, I didn't have to worry about becoming pregnant, seeing as it wasn't part of this particular process. In fact, it turns out that the Royal chooses when it's time for kids. It was quite handy and the part about Rafe going bareback was actually the main reason why we had only partially completed the matching process as of yet. Phases two and three were completed at the same time; by our true joining.

"Are you sure?" He nuzzled my cheek quickly and pulled away so he could look me in the eye.

"More than anything."

RAFE

At the peak of our climax, everything began to change. The marking on my back began to burn red with heat this time, instead of cool, and judging by the look on Payton's face, hers was doing the same. It was then I noticed the change in her eyes. They were now more of a purplish coloring. A surge of some kind had come over her though, causing her to writhe in pain, screaming, and I couldn't help the panic I felt.

What if something is going wrong?

"Payton?" I called out.

"I think I'm going to die!" she screamed, and as soon as her powerful surge of pain appeared, it seemed to vanish.

"Your eyes," she whispered, evidently shocked.

"What of them?" I asked.

"They're almost purple," she announced.

Matching eyes?

I smiled at that, holding her in my arms and dropping a chaste kiss on her lips. "So are yours."

"Holy shit! Really?" she said, then broke my grip to get out of bed and stand in front of the tall mirror in my bedroom's corner. Her eyes met mine in the mirror as she took in the marking on her shoulder blade. "Wow!"

"M-hmm." I admired her unabashed movements as she took in her changes before ordering her back to bed, to which she all too willingly obliged.

We lay in bed, holding each other when a knock came at the bedroom door. I looked at Payton, who nodded to let me know she was okay with me answering it.

"Go away!" I called instead, winking at her. She smirked, shaking her head at my antics. "We're busy." Taking her into my arms, I began to kiss her neck again, bringing forth a giggle. "If this is what I have to do to keep people away, I'll be damned if I ever stop."

Laughter trickled out of her at my statement.

"I'm not going to argue with you on that one," she whispered, nuzzling the side of my face with the side of hers. "Come in!"

"Are you decent?" It was my father.

Are you fucking kidding me?

"Seriously!" I chuckled with exasperation. "You have the worst timing. Hold on."

"I thought you'd be done by now," he called out. Payton quickly got up and slid her short white satin robe around herself before rushing back to the bed, covering her bare legs with the disheveled blankets, as I slid my underwear back on and opened the bedroom door. In walked Dad, who blushed immediately. I did the same thing, but I was confused as to why I felt embarrassed or even ended up reacting to his emotions at all. This hadn't been the first time Payton and I had gotten together under my folks' roof.

Payton studied my face, probably seeing my confusion. "What's wrong?" she asked.

"Why am I feeling embarrassed?" I asked.

My face crumbled, and I found myself registering anger. Moments later, that's when I noticed something was going on with Payton, as well, as I saw her ears perking up. It seemed as though Andy and Patrick were in the middle of an argument; something I doubted she would have normally heard.

"Did anyone just hear that?" she asked.

I looked at her in shock as I began to realize what was happening. "Hold on a minute!"

"What's going on?" Payton and I simultaneously asked, turning to look at my father.

"I see you've succeeded," he said.

Something told me he and Mom had known more about this whole Royal match thing than they had been letting on.

CHAPTER 10

PAYTON

What does he mean succeeded? I asked myself while he stared at the pair of us with a smirk, as if knowing a joke that Rafe and I had yet to catch on to.

Between hearing Rafe's brothers arguing downstairs, their mother trying to put an end to their feuding, and feeling frustration and anger with my empathic abilities, I was beginning to get a headache.

Rafe didn't seem like he was fairing much better either. He was growing pale and his fists were balled; knuckles white with the pressure of his own grip as he tried to deal with whatever he suddenly found himself being overwhelmed with. His eyes found mine as I watched him with worry. He reminded me of myself when I had first come into my empathic abilities. I knew from things Rafe had told me about his gifts that what I had found myself dealing with was similar to the abilities he had been born with.

But it can't be, can it?

Shaking the thought off, I realized I wasn't hearing Andy and Patrick arguing anymore. That in itself graced me with enough reprieve to gather my thoughts and begin processing all of this, while offering Rafe some tips and tricks.

I got up and rushed to my match, who seemed like he was about to start crying. I myself was feeling the emotion, but being too flustered with the rush to my other senses, I couldn't quite pinpoint where it was coming from. Yet with my experience, I was able to control its effect on my senses.

"Look at me," I told Rafe, standing in front of him. I grabbed his face between my palms as he did what I asked. "Breathe deeply and try to shut your mind from everything around you. Picture yourself building a wall between you and what you're feeling."

He closed his eyes and concentrated on it for a moment, using every tip I gave him; tricks I had learned from my father—the only one I'd ever known—biological or not. In the meantime, Sandra came into our room—hugging Will from behind—the air filling with a scent.

What the…arousal? Right now?

I looked wide-eyed to Will and Sandra, and my core began to warm slightly. I used my empathic abilities to feel exactly what I had smelled; yep, that's what it was all right.

Ugh…seriously? Who could be turned on at a time like this?

I looked back at Rafe and found him smirking at me as it appeared his struggles had calmed down, everything currently in check with him. Sandra stood in front of her husband, who now had his arms wrapped around her, hugging her tightly to him. I was still aware of the smell in the room, which was growing heavier and more pungent, and try as I might, I couldn't make its stench dissipate or ignore it in the slightest. As a matter-of-fact, the urge to jump Rafe was growing with each and every passing second. To give you an answer to my earlier question, apparently, I *could* be turned on at a time like this. Rafe lightly rubbed my arms soothingly, in an up and down motion, as they hung limp at my sides. I was slowly melting, and the last thing I needed was to go feral on this gorgeous piece of man who stood in front of me while his parents were right there. I felt like a bitch in heat.

My head snapped at Will, who was now chuckling; Sandra noticed the reprimanding look in my eyes and immediately tapped his arm so he'd stop.

"Explain," I ordered him in a slightly harsh and demanding tone. My head was spinning so much these days from all of these new discoveries; I was shocked I hadn't come down with a severe case of whiplash.

Under any other circumstance, I'd have said my eyes were deceiving me, but I could have sworn Will stood a little straighter at my commanding him to explain. I'm sure some day I'd laugh about all of this, but right now, I was freaked out to say the least, not to mention slightly insulted we hadn't been made aware of these new developments.

It just so happens that a Royal and her Royal Match exchanged their abilities and shared them once they'd succeeded at the bonding.

"I knew it worked when I came in and saw your eyes," Will stated. "You have the royal coloring in them now."

Rafe and I looked at each other over my shoulder as I sat on his lap, on the edge of our bed.

"A little warning about this power swap would have been good," I mumbled, as I felt Rafe's lips on my shoulder, breathing heated air through the satin of my bathrobe, a part of him very noticeably hard against my ass.

"This is part of what I mean about you getting stronger. Upon completing the bond, you and your match share each other's abilities," he explained. "No other Fae has the power to share abilities like you do, Payton."

"I'm not sure I'm enjoying this whole new scent, hearing, and sight thing, but I can see how handy they are for you guys." I smiled, feeling awkward.

"How you deal with this whole empathic thing is

beyond me," Rafe said into my neck, then bit it lightly. "I'm getting a headache already."

If he didn't stop, I'd be forced to turn around and take him there, in front of all to see. My raging hormones hadn't let up since smelling the arousal in the air earlier, and I knew Rafe was able to smell mine now. I squirmed a little deeper into his lap—as I tightened my thighs together—a feeble attempt at stifling this internal flame that was slowly being fanned. I should simply just get up and off of his lap, but I couldn't help but notice that my new and overwhelming senses relaxed some as soon as we made physical contact. It was kind of a no-brainer to remain semi-clear-headed, which is why I chose to stay where I was.

"Here." Will walked forward and dropped keys in Rafe's hand. I looked at the two men and Sandra in confusion. "You two clearly need some more time to get adjusted. The boys have left, and Sandra and I are due for some time alone. If you head out now, you can get to the cottage before midnight." With that, he followed Sandra out of the bedroom; some of the arousal scent left along with them, most of it remained.

RAFE

Half an hour later we were in my car, driving toward my family cottage. We were warned there were watchers around the property to keep an eye on us. So long as they stayed out of earshot, I was fine with it and made it known. I had plans for Payton and me, and the last thing I needed was to be disturbed. My breathing hitched at the thought of a few naughty things I wanted to try with her upon our arrival. My mouth watering at the fresh memory of her heated flesh against mine; the most intimate touch

I craved to have again and again. A hand rubbing up my thigh was what brought me back to reality. I turned to look at Payton, who eyed me curiously with an arched brow.

"You need to stop the thoughts you're thinking. You're driving me insane right now," she said in a husky tone, squirming in her seat.

Then suddenly, I had a picture invade my mind. My eyes still trained on Payton, I felt my blush wash through my entire body and my cock hardened. It was exactly what I had pictured doing to her, but with her very own twist added to it.

"What the hell was that?" I asked her, my cock so hard I wasn't sure I should be driving.

She laughed mischievously at my reaction. "I think we just found something new."

"I wonder if Dad knows about this one." I smirked, flashing a scene from earlier tonight of me wreaking pleasurable havoc on her body and cut it off as quickly as I heard the growl form in her throat. This had me grinning. The more I sat here thinking about our sharing of each other's abilities, the more I thought we could have fun with it. The mind link we apparently seemed to share was definitely an interesting plus.

PAYTON

The moon shone bright and high in the sky by the time we reached the Nottingham family cottage, nestled deep in the woods. Rafe had almost missed the dirt road that led up to it, as he veered quickly to the right, causing rocks, dirt, and other debris to kick up and a cloud of dust to float up in the air behind his car. I've never seen a man run as quickly as I had when he got out of the car, grabbed our bags, and tossed me over his shoulder like a sack of potatoes. He paused at the door to unlock it, and dropping our belongings inside, he locked the door behind us. Then he rushed up the stairs to one of the bedrooms as I laughed hysterically at his behavior.

"I can't help myself," he said, hovering above me once he had flung me onto the bed with a not-too-ladylike bounce. "That had to have been the longest drive of my life."

"Ditto," I whispered, electrical currents ran down to my toes with the scent of him filling my nose, causing images to flash through my mind. The throbbing in my core intensified, begging me to let go and allow him quench this thirst only he could satisfy.

I felt like I simply couldn't get enough of him—evidently Rafe was no better.

Other than showering and food, we spent the entirety of the next two days in bed, satisfying each other repeatedly, although, not entirely in a physical way per se.

Rafe had come up with an idea yesterday morning: he'd see how powerful our mind link could work. Let's just say, I woke up screaming his name in a fit of carnal bliss, which left me speechless when I realized it had all been in my head. My body begged to differ shortly afterward, when I found myself having to satiate my needs with his body, seeing as my core had throbbed and demanded for true physical release. I then returned that same favor when, to my delight, he was still sleeping when I woke this morning. His cock stood at attention for me as I began to pleasure him, sending sexy images through his mind. Yep, I was taking him to the next level—pleasuring both mental and physical all at once. He woke on the verge of exploding, throbbing in my grasp. All he could do was lay there, his eyes wide with blissful shock, looking into mine as he exploded in my mouth, moaning my name. To have watched the whole thing and not done anything to relieve the pressure inside as I played with him was a near impossible task. I ignored my urges, continuing to see my task through, impressed with my 'handy' work. Yes, pun intended.

It wasn't until we were heading back to Rafe's parents' residence when all hell broke loose. At first, it was the black SUV we'd driven by that had been pulled over to the side of the road: some guy fixing a flat. A few minutes up the same road—something struck me as odd—I had seen that SUV before. Sure, there were loads of black Chevrolet Suburbans with black-tinted windows out there, but something about this one looked familiar. I immediately wracked my brain, trying to figure out what exactly it was that struck a chord with me. All I came up with was the license plate. It read: B8DAVIS. It wasn't the vehicle per se, it was the damn plates on it that caused this sudden bundle of nerves to unravel and twist my stomach into a multitude of knots.

"Everything okay?" Rafe looked over at me, as I tried to avoid his gaze by staring out the window. I nodded. "I can smell your fear, Payton."

Damn. These abilities are killing me right now.

"I heard that too." He chuckled. "What's up, baby?"

"Drive faster," I told him.

"Why?"

"Because I think we're being followed," I said, this time meeting his eyes.

He took a quick look in his rearview mirror, and then I heard a deafening crash, which shot my head back into the headrest before it jerked forcefully forward toward the dash. My seat belt was the only thing keeping my body from flying out of my seat and sending burning pain across my chest from its movement restriction.

The rear windows of the car shattered as Rafe struggled to speed up and maintain control of the vehicle, the tires squealing on the pavement. The smell of fear was overwhelming inside the car—both his and mine. Thanking some higher power up above, I was glad when Rafe's sports car found purchase then jetted quickly forward. As I looked in my mirror, the Suburban had begun to fade away behind us. That's when I took notice of Rafe's cell phone, sitting in the console between the seats. My fingers fumbled over the screen to find his parents' number for an attempt to contact them. Never in my life had I been more thankful when someone picked up on the first ring at the other end.

"Help us!" I screamed. That's when a mix of colors waved across my vision, the feeling of weightlessness overcame me as the car Rafe and I were in was sent careening across the highway, onto the opposite side of the road. We went tumbling over and over again; heads over tails, into the ditch. The deafening sound of metal and plastic twisting and scraping on asphalt buried my screams of fear for my life—for Rafe's life. The phone I was holding was knocked out of my hands and must have landed to lie somewhere lost and out of reach.

When everything came to a stop, I looked over at Rafe to find him with an immense gash on his forehead, his eyes closed, but his breathing still detectable by the pulsing of a vein I saw on the side of his neck. The smell of smoke and gasoline was slowly making me feel nauseous. I heard the sound of car doors opening and closing in the distance. Panic began to settle in my gut again as I attempted to will it away with a few seconds of deep breathing.

I nudged Rafe and heard him groan. Unbuckling myself, I tried to turn my body toward him in an attempt to wake him up. Nothing prepared me for the blinding pain that seared through my right leg. After a heart-wrenching howl of agony, I looked down and saw the monstrous laceration in my thigh, with a piece of glass sticking out of it. I knew I was in trouble. I began hitting at Rafe, pleading with him to wake up.

"Rafe!" I yelled, feeling my strength escaping me. Maybe it was from blood loss, or an adrenaline dump; who knew?

The crunching of gravel and dirt underfoot dominated my hearing; I knew there was more than one person just by newly acquired heightened sense of smell. No sooner than that, I felt two sets of hands gripping me by the arms and ripping me out of the passenger side window.

"NOOOO! Rafe, please! Please, Rafe, wake up!" I shouted as loudly as I possibly could.

I turned to face one of the owners of those sets of hands and the blood rushed out of my face, ice filling my veins. I had been right the whole time. One of Matt's guys from the gym had me by the arm. The only things I remember from this point on was being shoved into the back of a Suburban, then seeing Rafe's eyes open, and his head turn toward me. Our gaze met for a split second as I felt a strike to the back of my head. The last things I heard after my vision had gone dark was a muffled howl and the sound of the back hatch shutting, then my senses left me altogether.

CHAPTER 11

PAYTON

I woke up—my injured leg burning—feeling like it was on fire. My head was pounding, and I hadn't a clue as to my whereabouts. The only thing I couldn't figure out was why I could have sworn I had heard Rafe calling my name, in an attempt to wake me. But when I opened my eyes, he wasn't there.

As I took in my surroundings, I realized I was in a beautiful room with floor-to-ceiling windows and thick velvety navy blue curtains. The bed I was currently lying on was comfortable and covered with silk sheets that were extremely soft. The comforter, also a dark navy, matched the curtains; and the four posters looked hand-carved. I heard the slight clicking of the doorknob turning and decided to feign sleeping, so I didn't have to deal with Matt or any of his minions.

I listened as I heard the very soft rustling of feet stopping directly beside me. Dainty hands pulled the sheets away from my body, and my eyes snapped open to see who it was that now delicately touching my thigh; my injured thigh in fact. I flinched and saw her jump a few feet back as I eyed her precariously.

"What are you doing?" I hissed, venom dripping from every syllable.

"I-I…" Her voice trailed meekly.

"You what?" I snapped, "Answer me!"

"I'm Kristy. He asked me to change your dressings," she explained, trembling with the fear she reeked of.

I couldn't help but think of how handy this whole newly acquired sense of smell was becoming. It turns out it was quicker to pick up a scent than trying to read someone with my empathic abilities, even after years of experience with them.

"*He?*" I eyed her.

"Master Davis," she mumbled, keeping her black irises trained to the floor submissively, avoiding eye contact with me completely.

"Master? He seriously makes you call him that?" I sneered, disgusted at the gall of this creep.

"That's right!" My head snapped up to the bedroom door where Matt Davis himself stood, arms crossed at his chest, and a smug look on his face. "Nice of you to finally join us."

I eyed him icily. "Not by my own volition, I can assure you," I ground through my teeth.

He stunk of confidence and condescension, but most of all, danger. The alarm bells were going off in my head nonstop. I knew I had to get out of here—but where was here? His house? A cottage? For all I knew, I could have been in a makeshift bedroom inside a freaking warehouse. *Or some dungeon. The man looks like he could have one of those with his sadistic nature.*

"You might not be here by choice now, but you will stay and do as I ask…in time." He paused as he came up beside me and tried to brush a strand of hair away from my face. I snapped my head away from his clutches, then smacked at his hand, which he easily grasped in his vice-like grip. He smirked at my fighting effort and the look of death I was giving him. "In time, you'll have forgotten about your dearest Rafe and his followers, and find your rightful place with me, at the forefront of this whole mess and in my bed." He attempted to kiss the top of the hand he still held hostage, but I ripped it out and gave it my best try as I swung into him for a punch he so aptly dodged.

Laughing, he turned his back on me and walked toward where he had come from. Pausing at the door, he looked over his shoulder at me.

"I like your feistiness. Making you scream is going to be fun." He chuckled eerily as he exited the room and shut the door behind him.

In your fucking dreams, bastard!

I woke to what I thought was Rafe's voice again. As I groggily cleared the fog from my mind, and let my eyes adjust to the lighting in the room, I took in my damning surroundings. I had hoped it had been nothing but a nightmare and that I was finally coming to in a bed—lying beside Rafe—but I was wrong. I knew I had to figure something out and quickly. Nothing good could come of Matt finding out that I was of royal descent.

I sat in bed, wondering about my man. Had Rafe gotten out of the car? Was he safe? Had his family come for us? The sweet sound of his voice still played around in my mind. As I thought of his voice, that's when it hit me like a ton of bricks.

The mind link!

True, only Rafe and I shared it, at least I thought that's how it was, seeing as we had yet to discover if it spanned further than that; but at least I'd be able to make sure everything was okay from their end. I hoped it would work, after all, it's not like we'd practiced our talents to their full extent and tested the distance limitations that may exist.

"Rafe?" I put all my energy into reaching him. I waited. Nothing… "Rafe, if you can hear me, please say something," I tried again. "I need you."

After a few more attempts, I was beside myself with hopelessness. I still hadn't managed to hear his voice inside my head. All I wanted—everything I searched for—was a sense of ease, of respite from this hellish ordeal. I wanted—no—I needed to know Rafe was safe. I needed to know he and the Nottingham crew were doing everything possible to get to me. Still, I couldn't fathom why it was I was able to hear Rafe through my sleep and not while conscious.

Or had I dreamed it all up?

I was snapped out of my reverie, of what I envisioned my reunion with Rafe being like, when I heard the click to the room's doorknob. I hoped with every fiber of my being it was Kristy but knew all too well that it would be too soon for one of her visits. I shifted defensively, pushing my back into the headboard as I stiffly sat up, my eyes seeing stars, and my head spinning from the sudden surge of burning pain in my thigh with my efforts.

Why couldn't I have superhuman healing powers with all these changes?

"Are you willing to submit yet?" Matt asked, a nasty smirk plastered to his lips.

"Drop dead!" I spat.

"I have to say, I love this feisty side of yours." He slowly approached the bed as if I was some kind of prey he was hunting. In all reality, I kind of was. "You'll make me one hell of a trophy when I'm done breaking you."

He tried to push my hair to the side as he inspected every square inch of exposed skin with his calloused fingertips. I didn't fight him this time, officially knowing he thrived on my earlier reaction. I wasn't about to give the brute any of what he was looking for. To say I was uncomfortable would be the understatement of a lifetime. Kristy had made me change into some satin baby doll number, which didn't leave much to the imagination, if you get my drift. Upon protesting, and with Kristy's help, I went through every single dresser drawer and the closet only to find piece after piece of lace, satin, and silk lingerie. The item I was currently wearing was the one I had deemed that possessed the most material to cover my body, and I still felt like I'd been dressed to be groomed as a member of the psycho's harem.

Matt ran his hard fingers down my cheekbones to my chin, as I shrank away from him; the headboard preventing me from disappearing altogether.

"I'm going to ruin you for any other," he stated softly and with boasting confidence. Those words sent icy shivers through my body and bile rising into my throat.

"I think I'm going to be sick," I managed, as I reached for his hand and threw it off of me.

All he did was click his tongue in disapproval at me and laugh at my reaction to his contact.

"You won't be able to keep away forever." He leaned into me, a hair's breadth away from my face, staring into my eyes maliciously. "I will have you. You'll need to decide if it'll be forcefully or willingly. Personally, I think a little force would be a delightful change for once."

With that, he pressed his kiss onto my unwilling lips.

"Payton, where are you?" I finally heard in my head, which made me gasp, giving the jackass the advantage and entry he saught.

Feelings of strength and relief overcame me. Attempting to push Matt away was futile. With anger rearing its ugly head, deep inside me, I bit his tongue as he tried to plunder my mouth to the point of my gagging. Matt's reaction was one I had expected. He screamed like a girl and bolted upright as I smirked; satisfied with the response I got from him. The only unexpected thing was the fist flying down onto my cheekbone, causing an instantaneous headache to rear its ugly head, along with dizzying stars and some lightly blurred vision.

"You'll regret that, bitch!" Matt's face was a deep crimson, his breath heavy with rage as he spat blood onto my bed coverings.

"Correction," I said. His mouth—opening as if to speak—but shutting as I glared up at him, my hand massaged my cheek and jaw. My teeth rattled but I couldn't care less about the pain, seeing as he kept wiping at his bloodied lip. I was determined to make it a living hell for him if he demanded my body as his possession. "*You'll* be regretting it, asshole!" I sneered, pouring every ounce of hate into those words, hoping he'd feel it seething into his soul.

He needs to clue in and leave me the fuck alone.

"Payton, please answer!" I heard Rafe.

"Please get me out of here," I cried out to him in my subconscious.

"Oh, thank fuck! Where are you?" he asked, relief lacing his every word.

"I don't know. I'm in some kind of bedroom," I told Rafe. Then growled a, "What?" at Matt, who had yet to leave the room.

He eyed me curiously. "What are you up to?"

"Where am I?" I demanded.

"Payton, answer me dammit!" Rafe said again in my head.

"Hold on, Rafe," I told my lover. "I'm dealing with a rather pissed off Matt right now."

"What's it matter? The case in point is I have you and you're not going anywhere," he answered, his rage replaced with a look of triumph. "You're all mine, baby, and I'll enjoy you every way I please." He turned to leave.

"They'll come for me!" I hollered at him, only to hear his booming laugh.

"They can try but they'll only fail," he said, as he closed the door behind him.

"I can't get anything from him," I told Rafe. "Where are you guys?"

He and I exchanged information. I was desperate to get the hell out of here and knew I couldn't do it on my own. I felt like I was grasping at strings that were always slightly out of reach. I know Rafe felt the same way I did.

We managed to rule out the Davis residence, their cottage, and various other properties of theirs. I was slowly losing hope that I'd be found. Just as I was promising Rafe I'd let him in on any new information I could manage to find, I heard the doorknob turn again.

"I think it might be Kristy," I announced.

"Who's she?" he questioned.

"A girl who's been taking care of my injuries," I explained.

"Use her," he said with determination.

"I have to go," I told him, as the door swung open and Kristy appeared. "I love you, Rafe."

"I love you. Be safe," he warned.

"Kristy, where are we exactly?" I asked her, when she was once again cleaning the sutures that held my wound closed before adding fresh gauze to my leg. I figured I'd start off with a direct hit, no use easing into it really.

"You know I can't tell you that," she said meekly. "I'm sorry, Payton."

Yeah, we were on a first name basis. That's what happens to two females stuck playing into Matt Davis' hand—you bonded over lingerie—despite how distasteful the shit was.

"Why not? We can help you," I told her.

She shook her head sadly in refusal. The look of fear, as well as defeat, on her face told me she was definitely not with the Davis clan of her own free will. Something kept her there, servicing their every whim, and I'm sure I couldn't fathom the extent of their extremist hold on her.

"I can't," she whispered. "If they were to find out, they'd kill me."

"Well, we're as good as dead here, anyway," I told her bluntly, pouting with my arms crossed at my chest, like your typical three year old, as she finished up with taping the gauze onto my leg. She looked up at me, trying to hide the fear that was blatantly obvious in her eyes. "You know he'll just kill us when he gets what he wants, right?" Perhaps instilling a substantial amount of fear for death in her mind, she'd be swayed to help. I needed her to see where I was coming from—where we were headed—if we kept playing Matt's game. She needed to see she had something better out there, something to live for—a happier life. "I found my match, Kristy. He can help us. If this is about–"

"I've got to go." She got up quickly and made for the door. "Make sure you eat your dinner tonight," she said, as she nodded toward the food tray that contained my earlier lunch in her arms. I could see the wheels turning behind those chocolate brown eyes of hers. As small as that reaction was, it was better than a full-on refusal to assist. "I'll be back before lights out with your dinner," she added, prior to shutting the door behind her.

I hadn't eaten since that meal Kristy helped me consume when I had first woken up after my arrival here, wherever here was. It was now Thursday morning—according to Kristy—and she had continued to come to check up on my bandages, my bruised cheek, and bring me breakfast.

A few seconds trickled by after she'd left my room, then I heard some yelling, a crash, and the scuffling of feet, followed by a few loud thuds in the hallway. It sounded as though it had come from directly in front of my room's door.

Please be okay, Kristy.

"You can't simply do anything right, can you?" A voice, which sounded like Matt's, bellowed through the door. I was proven right when the door slammed open and Mr. Almighty—himself—stormed in with a handful of the now stiff, cold porridge, I can only presume was from the tray Kristy had left with only minutes earlier. Walking up to me, he attempted to force his fistful of the stuff I regarded as poison down my throat. He quickly overpowered me with brute force, despite my attempts at shoving him off of me.

"Are you trying to die?" he hollered down at me. "You know I can arrange that. Hell, I'll even take care of you myself." I spat out the remainder of the porridge he had managed to push into my mouth, all over the front of his shirt. "I wonder what poor Rafe will say when I drop off your shriveled-up carcass on his doorstep when I'm done with you." He began to run his calloused hand over my injured thigh, squeezing it so I howled out in pain as he held my arms painfully in his other hand, up above my head.

The bastard!

He continued as he pushed my nightie up. I knew where this was heading, and I couldn't help the trembling my body was submitting to: my body betraying me completely in the sense it bared my fears for him to witness. I was terrified of the harsh reality Matt had so aptly painted before me, and I doubted starting to play his game now would save me in the end. This Neanderthal wasn't going to let me live—there was no chance in hell of that happening at this point. His fingers were only a few inches from the crease where my leg met my torso, when a throat clearing sound came from the door. With my head snapping up,

I looked through my tear-filled gaze to see one of Matt's minions smirking at us—the one that pulled me out of Rafe's car after the crash.

"Can I cop a feel?" he asked, amusement in his voice.

"What is it, Rob?" Matt growled at him, his gaze turned to the intruder, but his grip tightened even more over my injury.

"I need to know what you want me to do with the help," he said.

"Get her in here. She can clean the bitch up." Matt sneered down at me then released my leg. "Then, I'll have my fun with you, puppet." Leaning into me, he bit down hard on the soft skin above one of my breasts covered in barely-there lace. As I flinched, he licked the wound he inflicted, knowing it would most likely bruise. "Don't worry. I'll be back later to claim what's mine." Kristy rushed to my side with a swollen right eye and welt on her cheek. She helped me to sit up on the edge of the bed, shuffling my legs to the floor as I tried to regain control of my shaking body. "And Kristy, I need you to run an errand for me when you're done," Matt told her. "Remember your place because if you forget it again, I'll put you down like the dog that you are."

I collapsed into Kristy, letting out my monstrous sobs when Matt had finally closed the door behind him. She held me in silence for a few minutes until my control slowly came back.

"Shh." She patted my head, running her fingers through my hair in a soothing manner—much like a mother would a child.

"How could you let him do this?" I asked against her shoulder. "Don't you see that this is all wrong?"

"I know," she said, her voice shaking with emotion. I pulled away from her to look at her face. She was well on her way to shock. "I need you to eat this." She handed me an apple as she got up. "Then, you'll go get yourself cleaned up and changed. When I come back, I need you to be ready." I looked at her with confusion. The lack of food and drink for the last few days must have been getting to my head. I couldn't think straight, my abilities were practically shit at this point, all but my mind link with Rafe and some of my empathic abilities remained. I felt so defeated right then. Heeding Kristy's words, I decided to cave in to the constant rumbling my stomach was making and made quick use of the apple she had handed me.

Could she have really been hinting at helping me out?

I managed to carefully get my butt to the bathroom, which was adjoined to my room, cleaned the mess Matt had made of me, and changed into fresh clothes, if you can call them that.

"We're coming," I heard Rafe's sweet voice through our link, nearly an hour later.

"But how?" I asked.

"Kristy," he explained. "I need you ready to fight. We'll be there inside the hour; I hope."

"You hope?" I asked, my mind reeling. "I don't know how much more of this I can take, Rafe. Matt's coming back, and I don't think I can hold him off anymore."

"He better keep his hands off of you or so help me…" I could tell he was fully enraged at our plight. "We'll be there soon. I promise. I love you."

"I love you too. Please hurry."

CHAPTER 12

PAYTON

I was sitting on the edge of the bed when Matt came in again.

He smirked as I flinched, worried he might be aware of the coup Rafe was most likely staging against him. "Going somewhere?" Could Kristie have been found out?

"I wouldn't dream of it," I rebutted sarcastically on an eye roll.

"You're looking better," he stated, his eyes scanning my overall appearance, falling on the slight bruise that was beginning to appear around his teeth marks above my breast, which made him drool like the dog he was—a dog who deserved to be put down in the cruelest of fashion. The bastard was licking his chops with pride that he had left his mark on me. I felt like a well-seasoned piece of meat. He reeked of confidence and lust; something I had failed to detect over the course of the last few days, despite all too well knowing it was present. His attitude projected it enough without me having to try reading into his emotions, or sniffing him out, so to speak. I wasn't sure if it was the fact I knew help was coming, the food I had finally ingested, or if there were any other outstanding factors at play, but I was glad my various abilities were beginning to come back—perhaps it was a combination of all of the above. Excitement and desire seethed through his pores, furthermore invading my sense of smell, polluting the air I breathed as he slowly approached me; making bile rise in my throat. I got up to stand at his level, bearing most of my weight on my good leg, seeing as the other was pretty much useless. I needed to assume a position of equality, not of lesser power like the bed would ensure.

Save your energy, Payton.

I knew I'd need that leg sooner rather than later if I managed to get out of there, but there was no way I was going to sit if the man before me wouldn't.

Come on, Rafe! I thought to myself.

"Stay back!" I ordered him, holding his gaze with a glare.

His eyes danced playfully as he attempted to close the gap between our bodies. "What's the little bad succubus going to do?" he taunted, as he matched my every step.

I brought my arms up in front of me, hoping I could halt his progress, but all he did was grab them roughly and push me back, making me land on my back, on the bed. I tried to scramble up the sheets, toward the headboard, attempting to find a way out of his advance. I needed to buy time until Rafe got there.

"This is going to be fun." He gave me his trademark cocky grin as he backed off the bed and began to unbuckle his belt.

I so desperately craved for the day I would be able to wipe that smug look off of his ugly face; this spanning since the day I had met him in the gym. I hoped today was going to be the day I did just that.

"You will regret this," I warned him in my most confident voice, my eyes trying to dig deep within him, to see if I could find a slight hint of humanity in the monster. I needed to see some compassion, some pity, just something that would help me in slowing him down or altogether stop him. There was nothing. "I promise you that," I added, my voice holding strong. This only seemed to humor him.

"You can keep your promises." He chuckled smugly. "Have I ever told you how magnetic you are? I bet you your kisses are deadly."

"Want to find out?" I smirked; the idea of me sucking his life force from his body was incredibly appealing at the moment. Maybe my ability could be channeled to do as I wished, instead of simply me being passive to them? It would be great if I could call upon that very ability when I needed it most. That's when I swore if the guy kissed me again by force, I'd make it my life's mission to control my succubus ways in the cruelest of aims.

I knew it wasn't necessarily the best time to be a smartass with him, but if Matt wanted to play a cunning, rough game; I was more than willing to oblige him. At some point, he'd be bound to slip up and leave his guard down, which would allow me to gain the upper hand. If I succeeded at knocking him out with my succubus charms, then I would, but I knew not to rely on simply that. He knew of my capabilities, and I doubted he was as stupid as Gage to make a mistake that could jeopardize his plans; a mistake like kissing a succubus on the mouth. My only defense was purely physical—my feminine wiles were undoubtedly ineffective. I'd been too clear with my disgust of him, and he didn't seem to be the type to fall at a woman's mercy—more like the man to assume full dominance at every turn.

I never thought there would be a day I would be starring in my very own horror movie, yet here I was. Matt had me pinned against the sheets, binding my arms to the headboard before he began trailing hard, rough kisses, not to mention, painful bites across the skin on my neck and chest. He managed to rip the nightie I had been wearing, leaving me bare-chested and painfully exposed to his aggressive advances.

"You taste delicious, puppet," he mumbled against my skin.

My arms were progressively getting weaker as I found myself struggling against the restraints. I was really in a pickle now with my being tied down and having only one good leg to defend myself with. My physical options were pretty much damned, my escape options were all exhausted, if I had to be frank in this moment. Rafe couldn't get here soon enough. Matt's hands found their way quickly to the edge of my underwear and began tugging at them. My blood ran cold.

"Please don't," I pleaded, unable to control my tears of helplessness.

This was the beginning of the end I had resolved myself to believe wouldn't happen. The surge of emotion I was feeling was off-putting, seeing as my walls were crumbled. I was dealing with the feelings of Matt's excitation, sexual thrill, elation, and relief that he was winning at breaking me, along with my own lengthy list. I found myself wondering what he would think, say, and do; once he figured out he couldn't take the power he lusted after unless he killed me. Not now that I was fully matched with Rafe. I shuddered at the thought of never seeing my love again.

"Payton, hold tight," I heard internally from Rafe.

I wasn't going anywhere, that's for sure.

"Please hurry," I cried inside my head. "I-I…He's…" My voice trailed away in my mind as tears stung my eyes, continuing to boil over onto my face. I couldn't bring myself to finish the thought. Oh, how I wished Rafe never had to walk in on this scene.

"I said don't!" I hollered at Matt with whatever last ounce of resolve I had remaining within my soul, trying to buck him off of my torso, which he was now straddling. It hurt my injured leg like a bitch, but I no longer cared. My movement only tilted him off balance slightly, and he recovered just as quickly as it happened, only for him to punch me in my already bruised cheek again, before he wrapped his hand around my throat, air barely making its way through to my lungs.

"You like it rough, huh?" He laughed to himself. "Let's see if you like it when I tear your insides out with my dick." His eyes, filled with pure evil, instilled the fear of God in me, but the one emotion that ran deeper than my fear, the one that took me almost off guard was rage. It was borderline out of this world and it unsettled me to no end.

"I said NO!" I commanded, my eyes holding his, my head pounding as I suddenly felt heat emanating from my sockets. Matt froze over me, and that's when I heard the sweetest sound in the world. Terrifying as this commotion was, it was definitely the most welcomed symphony of my entire existence at this point.

The noises got progressively louder with every passing second. Matt was still frozen above me as I held his gaze, the burning in my eyes easing slowly while my instantaneous headache receded until they both had finally disappeared altogether, and I gained full control of my power of command.

"Your eyes! They're…" He gasped. "It can't be…" His voice trailed.

"You will remove yourself from this bed this instant!" I ordered.

He shook his head abruptly in an attempt to snap himself out of my hypnotic gaze but couldn't. Shock might have been a factor for him, because in the next second, he uttered, "Well fuck! A matched Royal."

Then the door to my room smashed open.

The cavalry had arrived.

CHAPTER 13

PAYTON

It all happened so fast. The door to the bedroom flew open, and my own feelings of relief, joy, and apprehension became quite overwhelming, superseding the feelings of those belonging to everyone in my vicinity prior to my room being charged into.

"Back the fuck off of my woman!" Rafe growled. "Payton, are you okay?" he added, his voice conveying his worry but predominantly relief.

"Y-yeah," I stammered, my mind now registering the fact I was still bare for anyone and everyone to see if they walked in.

I pulled myself up with what strength remained in my arms, pushing myself up the bed with my one good leg, but no matter what I did, I couldn't manage to shift my torn negligee to cover my chest up—it would have to wait until someone undid my bindings.

"How sweet," Matt began in a singsong tone, as he slowly backed away and off the bed to stand at its foot, remaining as a barrier between Rafe and I.

I could hear light scuffling out in the hallway again and

knew by the self-assured smirk on Rafe's face that his plan had worked.

RAFE

I stood over Matt, satisfied of the beating I had handed him. The guy lay sprawled on the floor, blood coming from his mouth and oozing out of his nose, his breath ragged. Much to my dismay, he was still very much alive and would survive just fine—at my father's boss's request of course. I had never really approved of violence that resulted with death, but to be frank, I truly did wish Matt Davis dead for all he had done. Especially for the horrors he had brought upon us—mostly for those brought onto Payton.

The noises from the hallway had completely died down once again, and in came Andy and Patrick—beaten and disheveled—but otherwise in great spirits. One look in Payton's direction, however, and their eyes averted their gaze immediately up to the ceiling, where they remained.

"Um, Rafe?" Patrick started nervously.

"What?" I snarled still breathing heavily as I remained towering over Matt's crumpled and unconscious form. I was still trying to regain full control over the rage I had taken out on Payton's kidnapper only moments ago.

"Uh…you might want to…uh." Patrick gulped.

What the fuck is wrong with these two?

"Would you just spit it out already?" I demanded in an exasperated tone, and turned to look at my brothers and with my eyes, looking up toward the direction their gazes had taken. "What the fuck are you two doing?" Both guys pointed in Payton's direction, as they then turned their backs to her. When I followed their silent directive, I cursed myself for being so blinded by my emotions. "Someone get her some clothes!" I ordered no one in particular, then rushed to her side.

"No, don't! I'd rather wear these sheets, if anything," she told me, blushing.

"Holy shit!" Andy exclaimed as he peered into the closet.

"I second that," Patrick added, as he took in the dresser's selections.

As for me, I refused to look away from Payton as I finished untying her arms, massaging her torn up wrists, and looking her over for any signs of injury. Fuming at the bruises on her face, I then winced at the bandage on her leg.

"Are they numb?" I asked, to which she nodded.

I continued to massage and get as much blood circulation back into her limbs with the least amount of discomfort. Next, I stripped myself of my T-shirt then pulled the ripped lingerie off of her upper torso, before pulling my shirt over her head, letting her string her arms through their respective holes.

Taking a moment, Payton leaned into my neck and took a long sniff. The quaking in her body seemed to dull a little. I was pleased I could offer her comfort in such an easy manner. To be frank, she offered it right back to me without even knowing it.

Wrapping her in one of the sheets, I picked Payton up and carried her out of the room that had been her prison for the last four days. I only wished the horrors could stay buried there, but I knew that it was easier said than done. Unfortunately, problems always have a way of following us—her in particular. Payton's past was more than enough to prove that statement true.

I'll have to make a point in changing that.

PAYTON

Morning had come too quickly. I woke with strong arms wrapped snuggly around me, Rafe's body pressed against the front of mine, soft fingertips rubbing soothing circles on my side as I tried to melt further into him. Security was the one sensation that dominated my senses in the moment.

"I thought I lost you," I mumbled into the kiss I had just deposited onto his chest, my arms sneaking around his torso, pulling myself further into his warmth.

On our way home, I had been quite incoherent through most of the drive, due to adrenalin drop, and by the time we arrived at our destination, I had fallen into some kind of unconscious state I hadn't woken from until just now.

"You can't lose me. Not that easily," he whispered against my forehead and kissed it tenderly. "Now sleep. We're spending the day in bed."

"You would think I'd be sick of being in bed." I chuckled at the less than fond memory of my four days of captivity.

Anyone who was sane could have easily made the assumption I had lost my marbles from post-traumatic shock. Those who knew me well would know I was from the school of if-you-can't-find-humor-out-of-any-situation-what's-the-point-in-living. Rafe looked at me with darkness in his eyes, not finding my dark humor all that amusing. He was pained. I knew he blamed himself, but the one person to blame in all of this was left spilling his blood on the floor of my former prison last night.

"But I'd take hundreds more of those days if they were all with you," I added, in time to see the genuine smile that formed on his lips.

The next few days had been the toughest by far. As promised, Rafe and I spent all of Friday in our room. He hadn't left my side since bringing me home, and I mean that quite literally. Answering calls of nature was the only exception. Heck, he had gotten Sandra to come in and bring us food if he couldn't do it himself, due to his anxiety about parting from me. She humored him, acknowledging her motherly instincts, and seeing it as the only way she could check up on me, since I'd refused to see anyone but Rafe until today.

I struggled with trying to get back on my feet, sorting through various emotional set-backs—which I knew wouldn't fade away for a very long time, if ever—along with filling the Nottinghams in on what I had been sub-jected to. They were disgusted by my treatment to say the least, as the picture I painted for each and every one of them was quite a grim and disturbing one. I couldn't help but notice Patrick and Kristy being quite chummy with each other when Rafe and I had made our first appearance on Saturday morning for breakfast. I was glad she had managed to escape more or less unscathed. Most im-portantly, the Nottinghams had welcomed her with open arms. I would be forever indebted to her for her valiant help. She didn't have to risk her neck for me but she had. I mean, she didn't know me from Eve and had no alle-giances toward me but had still pulled through. Kristy turned out to be a great source of information for us, and we couldn't be happier to have her as one of our own. We knew the war of the Fae world was literally upon us. There was no longer any time for training. We were staring this possibly suicidal trek directly in its face. Personally, I felt like I was standing on the edge of some damning precipice. There was no turning back now; not after my kidnapping, and certainly not now we'd managed to infiltrate enemy territory so I could be saved.

And now I'm expected to lead us into this new Fae world we're trying to shape?

I wished Will hadn't reminded me of this fact so soon, but reality waits for no one. Uncertainty in my capability of leadership was definitely bound to keep me awake tonight and for many nights to come.

THE END

ABOUT THE AUTHOR

Born and raised in small town Northern Ontario, Canada, Carey Decevito has always had a penchant for reading and writing.

More than a decade later, with weeks of sleepless nights, she finally gave in and put pen to paper (more like fingers to keyboard!) She submitted to the dreams that plagued her. And the rest, as they say, is history!

A member of the RWA, Carey enjoys spending time with family and friends, the outdoors, travelling, and playing tourist in Canada's National Capital region. When life gets crazy, this contemporary erotic romance author seeks respite through her writing and reading. If all else fails, she knows there's never a dull moment with her two daughters, her goofy husband, and cat and dog who she swears are out to get her.

She is the author of both *The Broken Men Chronicles, Nightshade* and *Essence Extracted* series.

CONNECT ONLINE

Website – www.careydecevito.com
Email – carey.decevito@gmail.com
Facebook – http://www.facebook.com/carey.writes

ALSO BY CAREY DECEVITO

The Broken Men Chronicles series

Once Written, Twice Shy
Almost Forgotten
Play Me to Infinity
To Forgive & Hold Safe
A Heart's War

Nightshade series
Night Break
Night Shift

Essence Extracted Trilogy
Essence Derived
Essence Surfaced

night break

nightSHADE

CAREY DECEVITO

PROLOGUE

DALTON

One Year Ago...

If I had to deliver that fucker's obituary, this is how it would read:

Rick Donnelly—Wannabe war hero, traitor, terrorist. May he burn in hell.

In truth, he was the scum who managed to kidnap my friend Theo Lowell's nephew, Jasper, then made off with the man's woman, all for the sake of petty revenge and furthering his stance in organized crime.

Now, he was nothing but a piece of shit, sprawled forward, split in half, and wedged between Warehouse Ten and the front end of Theo's brother's pickup truck.

Dead.

Collapsing to my back, Theo held onto his woman, Morgan, at my side. Allowing a long, drawn-out breath to escape, it helped ease the tension in my body as I dealt with the pain in my hand and leg. The damn bastard might be dead, but he did some damage before Morgan drove a truck straight through him. My shooting hand now had a hole through it, and since I was reaching for the gun in my ankle holster at the time, the fucking bullet managed to hit my bad knee.

It's over. Thank God for crazy-assed women, great friends…and random strangers.

Jasper was safe.

Morgan was safe.

And Theo could settle into the life he thought he'd all but lost only hours before.

Sounding on the verge of tears, he uttered, "Huss?"

With our adrenaline dropping from the night's festivities, I couldn't blame his emotional state. The same gamut of emotions was reeling through me too, and I hadn't had to track down two loved ones, nor had I had the displeasure of being held hostage, having to free myself, then do the same for the woman I loved. All this with some unknown cyber vigilante, who'd popped out of nowhere, to help him out. One we'd been forced to have blind faith in.

I'm your girl, Mr. T.

Yeah, Hussy was our girl tonight. Definitely.

"Yeah?" she said through that voice distorter of hers.

"Thank you." Theo's voice lodged in his throat, leaving the man incapable to add to his words.

It took a few seconds to get a response, but when it came, albeit in that robotically masculine voice again, it was just as overwrought with the same jumble of emotion that Theo and I seemed to be experiencing. "You're welcome, Mr. T," she whispered.

Hussy's earlier concerned outburst to my being shot jumped to the forefront of my mind. This spurred me into action. I didn't know why I felt compelled to reassure her, but I found myself unable to stop myself from doing it. Hussy wasn't one of my team at Nightshade Security, yet tonight, she had come through for all of us. Despite never having met, a bond had been forged between the team, Hussy, and myself. Plus, I've always been one to listen to my gut, and it's proven me right every time, so it was why I said what I did next.

"Huss?" I managed.

Her distorted voice caught. "Yeah?"

"I'll be fine." I swallowed the ball of emotion that had made my voice come out sounding like gravel. "But I'm going to need your name, honey."

What I got next was an unaltered, breathless sounding, "Kip," that made my lungs seize, my body tighten, and a part of my anatomy take notice in a very visceral way.

I had no idea who this woman was. She'd only spoken a single word—the nickname she'd given me based on my last name—Kippers. But that's all I needed. I can't explain the electrical charge that rolled through me, or the sense that something greater was at play. I simply needed more of that voice. I needed more of *her*. "I want to know—"

I heard a subtle thump on the other end of the line, followed by a long sigh.

I never thought that a sigh could hold so much untold emotion, but hers did.

Exhaustion.

Wistfulness.

Hesitation.

Defeat.

Fear.

"Don't," she whispered, and I could have sworn I'd heard her add a "please" to that. "Let's just leave it at this." I didn't want to. A gnawing feeling in my gut told me that I needed her still; that I wanted her. "I only did what needed to be done. It's what I do."

Something told me that pushing her right then would be ineffective, so I gave in, much to my displeasure. But I did it in a way that left the proverbial door open and the ball in her court. "Okay, Huss. If you ever need anything—"

I could tell that she was contemplating my words. "I won't." The tone of finality in those words had disappointment weighing me down until she continued, "Tell you what, I'll be in touch if something ever comes up."

Disappointment fled and hope took its place. This was as good as I was going to get. "Okay."

Silence dominated the next ten seconds before Hussy broke it. "I'm going to sign off now."

"Huss?" I was desperate and I didn't care. I wanted to reach through the communication device shoved in my ear canal and yank her to where I lay, so I could see the face that belonged to the voice. I wanted to figure out why she was how she was, what made her tick, what set her off. Hell, I'd have been happy to wait out the medics and the slew of first responders with her voice in my ear, telling me everything was going to be okay, just like Theo was doing with Morgan.

But before I could do or say anything, the line went dead, all coms were down, and sirens could be heard in the distance.

I could feel Theo's gaze aimed at the side of my face. He probably wanted to know what the fuck was going on with me.

Ignoring the man, I thumped my head onto the dock in sheer frustration, and closed my eyes. "Bye, Huss," I whispered.

CHAPTER 1

DEVOLIN

Present Day...

Come on. Come on. Come on!

"Come. *On!*" I bounced in place as I watched the progress bar run its course, and then punched the air in victory once it hit one-hundred-percent. "Gotcha!"

Disconnecting the thumb drive from my laptop, and slamming the top down on it, I scooted out of bed and proceeded to stuff the lot into my satchel.

There was no other option than to go straight to *him*.

This was life or death, and everything hinged on what I did next. I'd long since made a promise to myself that I'd never risk making contact with the team I'd bonded with after one night of mayhem. But promise or not, this information I'd just dug up wasn't something I could relay to him over the phone.

It needed to be seen.

Analyzed.

Discussed.

That meant that I needed to see Dalton Kippers. In the flesh. Talk to him. Show him what I'd found, what he was in for.

Then, I needed to get far away from him, and move on already, because this crazy obsession I had developed over the man was getting out of hand. My best friend, Skylar, had told me as much on multiple occasions. And when Skylar deemed it fit to force her wisdom upon me, I needed to listen. It's been nearly a year since I helped Dalton and his team rescue Jasper Lowell and Morgan Smyth for Christ's sake!

On a snort, I shrugged off where my thoughts were heading and closed my bag.

"What are you doing?"

The breath in my lungs seized. "Sky!" Hand clutched at my chest, I turned to face the woman, waiting for my erratic heartbeat to calm. "You scared the living shit out of me."

Skylar leaned against the doorjamb, dressed in wrinkled hot pink scrubs from a hard day's work, smirking. "Well, at least we know one of us is capable of getting that ticker of yours up above a slow trot now, don't we?" She breezed into the room, nodded toward my satchel, a glimmer of curiosity entering her gaze. "What's going on?"

I bit my bottom lip, knowing the guilt showed on my face for what I was about to ask of my dearest friend. Then I blurted, "Sky, I need your help."

"Do I need to worry that the cops will be coming in here to cart your ass off to jail?" she asked.

"I need to get out of here for a few hours."

"Dev, you know I can't—"

"It's life or death, Sky."

Skylar's eyes widened. "Dev, what in the hell have you gotten yourself into?"

I headed toward the cabinet, that passed itself off as a closet, and grabbed the pair of jeans and t-shirt I'd been wearing when I had been admitted. My irritation at the lack of immediate support showed with each jerky movement I made. "Can you or can't you help me out?" I turned to look at her from over my shoulder.

Skylar crossed her arms over her chest, taking a seat in the chair closest to my hospital bed. "You look flushed. How're you feeling, and tell me the truth."

Oh no, not that no-nonsense tone of hers. If I told my friend, who incidentally was a nurse, that I was feeling 'off' for lack of a better description, there'd be no way Skylar would let me walk out of there, say nothing of her covering for my absence with Doris, the nurse that was currently on duty. Damn woman was so old, she should have retired a decade ago, but seemed to find it amusing to torture her patients. That's why Skylar and I had dubbed her Nurse Battle-Axe. Because of this, and the fact that I did need to get out of there, I went with, "I'm fine," and hoped that my bad acting, let alone lying skills wouldn't give me away.

Unfortunately, the lack of conviction my words held, and the pause I had to take to brace myself against the wall to wait out the wave of dizziness that hit me, didn't help my cause.

"Uh-huh…"

"I'm not kidding, Sky. I need to do this." I whipped my pajama top off and flung it at the bed, slipping my shirt on. "This case…it's *big.*"

"Dev—"

"No!" I persisted, yanking down my pajama bottoms, then headed to the bed for needed support. Leaning on it, I slid my legs into my jeans, wiggling them up over my ample hips. "*He*'s in danger, Sky."

Her eyes rounded as realization hit her. "He, as in *he*?" I nodded. "I thought we'd discussed this, Dev." She sighed.

"No, *you* discussed it. I merely listened. You told me to move on and I will. Just…" My frustration came out in a huff. "I have to see this through. It's my fault he took this case in the first place, so by default, it's my responsibility to make sure he knows what he's heading into. The people he'll be dealing with…" Another sigh accompanied my shake of the head. "They're not good, Sky."

"Okay." Skylar paused mid-thought. "Say I let you leave. How the hell am I supposed to keep Doris out of here?"

"She knows you come in here after your shifts. She never bothers to check in on me when you're here, you know that."

"So you want me to…?" She let her words hang so I could fill the gap.

"I know it's not right for me to ask this of you, but can you stay here, as in this room, until I get back?" Biting my lip in that nervous tick of mine, I continued, "And I'll need your keycard."

"Devolin!" she scolded.

Both of us looked toward the room's door and listened for a short moment to see if Skylar's outburst had generated some attention.

"I'll take the back way out and come in the same way. The emergency stairwell is just outside that door."

"I can get fired for that," she whisper-yelled, shooting the door another glance. Still, the woman pulled her access pass and handed it over.

I snapped it up from her hand then shrugged. "Just say you lost it if anyone asks."

"Yeah, yeah. You're lucky I love you, woman," she grumbled.

Knowing I had her where I wanted her, I grinned. "So you'll help me out?"

On a curt nod, Skylar got to her feet. "Yeah." Her eyes did a full head to toe appraisal before she shared my smile. "But we need to do something about your hair and makeup first."

I blew out a relieved sigh, hoping my eyes conveyed my appreciation. I really would have left against hospital advice—sure, I'd return after my duty was done—because a life, if not lives, hung in the balance and it was all my fault.

Sneaking out of my room, and down the stairwell, proved to be easy enough. Nurse Battle-Axe was out on the floor and away from the nurses' station. Heading down two floors, I exited the stairs, and made my way toward the bank of elevators that would take me the rest of the way down to the main lobby. When I got there, I jumped in the first cab that I spotted, rattling off my home address.

Upon my arrival, adrenaline running at an all-time high, I hurried to my vehicle. Finding it parked in its usual spot of my mother's garage, I noticed the bay next to it was empty and thanked the powers up above that I wouldn't have to deal with dear old Mom right away.

Hitting the fob, I opened the door, dropped my bag on the passenger seat, then settled into the driver's side.

"Hello, baby," I cooed to my newest acquisition, the leather upholstered finish and new car smell that had yet to fade, even after nearly a year of ownership.

Hitting the button that would open my bay's door from the controller on my visor, I put the key in the ignition and turned it. Sending my destination from my phone to the car's GPS, I took a few short seconds to enjoy the purr of the Charger's engine. Then I shifted my ride into reverse.

Nightshade Security Investigations—Dalton's company—was closed, so I made my way to the former corporal's home to find that it too lacked the one man I was trying to locate. I did take the time to admire the two rockers on his front wraparound porch and the American flag hanging in a place of pride on one of the support pillars framing the steps.

I hope I'm not too late.

I wasn't sure what I'd do if Dalton had already skipped town. Just as quickly as that thought popped into my head, another followed it.

Theo would know where he is.

Reprogramming my GPS for Theo and Morgan's place, I reared out of the drive and floored the gas pedal. Fifteen minutes later, my lead foot caused me to nearly miss the entry to the driveway, as I reached my third, and hopefully, final destination.

It wasn't until my finger released the doorbell that I realized how truly horrible I was feeling. To make matters worse, my nerves had also kicked in, and I had a fleeting thought that perhaps I should have given myself a quick cursory glance in the mirror before exiting the car. There were no do-overs on first meetings, after all, and I was about to meet more than just Theo and possibly Morgan today, seeing as it looked to be that they had a visitor, judging by the third vehicle parked at the front of the house.

As luck would have it, someone was home.

I would have cried out my relief at the sight of the pregnant woman before me, but a whispered, "Morgan," was the only thing I could muster as soon as the door opened.

The woman's eyebrows furrowed in apparent confusion. "Do I know you?"

I shook my head, indicating the negative, because that's all I could do. I was too busy fighting the sudden bout of nausea and dizzying heat. Next thing I knew, my vision tilted, then dimmed, and my knees gave out.

At the feel of a cool damp rag sponged against the hollow of my throat, over my forehead, my cheeks, and then back again, some of my faculties returned. The sensation was like heaven on my overheated skin. I sighed at the same time a, "Mr. T," escaped me.

"W-what, did she say?" I recognized Dalton's voice immediately. Unable to get my eyes to cooperate and open, I heard a thump come from right beside me, accompanied by the heat of another body warming the side of my torso.

"Danger…Kip," I mumbled, and then everything started to fade again.

Before I was able to embrace the darkness that swooped in, I felt the palm of Dalton's callused hand gently cup my cheek as he whispered, "Huss?"

CHAPTER 2

DALTON

With a lot of convincing to get the medics to allow me to be there, here I was, sitting in the back of an ambulance with who I suspected was Hussy, the cyber ghost I'd set Brycen to tracking in his spare time over the last year.

Her name: Devolin Payton Taylor. At least that's what the ID in her bag said when I managed to sneak a look at it after the paramedics had located it. I wouldn't be surprised if she'd faked her own identity, seeing as she seemed hell-bent on remaining anonymous.

Leaning forward onto my knees, I peered at the woman splayed out onto the gurney before me. Out cold.

Morgan had told me that Hussy looked panicked when she first opened the door to the woman. Then she'd collapsed and Theo had called 911. Morgan rushed to get me a cold cloth, and I'd been left with an unconscious woman. Her head rested in my lap, as I tried to decipher what her few short words meant, and why she'd chosen now to show herself.

Devolin whimpered in her sleep, causing me to reach out and grab the hand closest to me. Her very tiny, dainty, exceptionally soft hand.

My eyes trailed up from her digits, her arm, her shoulder, the delicate neck that held a thrumming but steady pulse, to her face. Her license said she had green eyes, but

I wondered if they'd shimmer like emeralds, taper closer to the hazel side of things, or would be bright like aquamarines. Beyond that, her lips were full, dark pink, almost rosy, reminding me of bubble gum. A fleeting curiosity of if she'd taste as such washed over me, but I shrugged it off. It was her hair that had me begging to set it free and run my fingers through it. It was a deep auburn, with streaks of darker reddish hues mixed in. Her skin was pale, but I knew, with the small line of freckles over the bridge of her cute nose, that her complexion wasn't that much darker when she wasn't ill, as she seemed to be now.

What the fuck is the matter with you? Scolding myself internally for waxing poetic about an unconscious woman, one I'd had a past with, yet had never met before. I bowed my head, trying to devise a plan of action, now that I had bullied my way into being by her side.

DEVOLIN

I woke up in what looked like the back of an ambulance, my hand clutched in a firm and warm grasp.

Allowing my head to drop sideways, I found myself looking at Dalton, who sat beside me. His head was bent forward. He was leaning onto his knees, one of them bouncing out of what I surmised was anxiety. I can only imagine what went through his, Theo's, and Morgan's heads when here I had shown up out of nowhere, and then before I could explain anything, I pulled a Sleeping Beauty maneuver on their asses. That thought had me rolling my eyes, cringing internally.

Dalton had yet to notice that I'd woken up, so I took the opportunity for a more thorough perusal of the unguarded man before me while I had it.

His dark brown, almost black hair was due for a cut,

slightly falling over his eyes. I wondered how it would feel between my fingers if I were to brush it away. Dalton had a chiseled jaw with a slight square shape, full lips, strong and masculine features that guaranteed him to look mean one minute, yet soft when the time called. His nose had a slight bend to it, most likely from combat, as with the small scar on the side of his right cheek, by his hairline. I could only assume since I'd been unable to access most but not all of his service records. He looked infinitely better in person than in any of the photos I'd dug up. Trust me, I'd searched those babies out, if only to indulge in my insane obsession over a man I've never met, but had spoken with once.

Damn!

Dalton must have sensed that I was conscious for his head shot up and his steel grey eyes connected with mine. "You're awake." The silk of his voice ran over me, goosebumps exploding on my skin, making me withdraw my hand from his so I wouldn't give myself, or my reaction to him, away.

Double damn! Wait; was that my voice? Embarrassment filled me as a grin broke over his face, solidifying the fact that I had spoken aloud. But that look though… Had I felt anywhere close to one-hundred-percent, that look on his face would have melted my panties. I'm sure of it.

As it was, my mouth had gone dry, my tongue feeling as if it had tripled in size. "Uh."

"If you're going to look, I'd rather you be doing it while I can watch." His grin transformed into a smile.

My mouth opened for a rebuttal to his bold statement, then closed because words evaded me.

Light danced in the man's eyes. "The jig is up, Huss." His words were filled with pride. "Or should I say Devolin Payton Taylor?"

"How'd?" He patted my hand then twined his fingers

through mine, setting off another set of goosebumps, but I knew how he found out. "You went through my stuff."

He followed his curt nod with, "How are you feeling?"

I tried to pry my hand from his like before, but he didn't give this time. "Where's my bag? I—I need to show you something."

"I asked you a question, Devolin."

I pulled at my hand again. Stuck. "Just let me—"

Instead of the gentle tone he'd led with, this time, his words brokered no argument. All alpha-like. "Don't. Brush. Me. Off, Devolin."

"But—" My words ceased halfway out of my mouth as his lips formed a thin line in warning, his hand squeezing mine as an added measure.

I tried to lift my head, but collapsed back onto the stretcher's pillow as the nausea and dizziness, that had been absent since my waking, set in again. For the first time to-day, I started to really worry. This was all too reminiscent. Closing my eyes, I begged. *Please don't let it be back. I can't deal with this right now.*

"What is it?"

My eyes snapped open. The paramedics had to have given me drugs or something. It could be the only reason why I couldn't keep my thoughts to myself.

Dalton leaned closer, the squeeze on my hand a gentle one. "What's back? What's the matter? Come on, Dev, talk to me."

He couldn't know. I didn't want him to know. I was there simply because I felt responsible in warning him, to keep him and his team at NSI safe. I should have known that exploring my connection with Dalton couldn't lead to… And what was it that I wanted it to lead to? A happily ever after? I snorted at the thought then averted his quest-ing gaze by turning my head to look up at the ambulance's ceiling. No, there would be none of that romance book nonsense for me. If I was having a relapse of some kind, this solidified why I had to push him away. I was best off making sure he had what he needed for that case of his; then disappearing from his life like I'd done the first go around.

Impatience clearly showing, Dalton groaned, "Devolin."

I closed my eyes, soaking in the warmth growing inside me, all due to the sound of his voice. Trying to breathe away my nausea, I silently prayed he'd say my name again. "You smell good. Like soap, mint, and man," I whispered.

"Devolin." He sounded humored.

I chose to ignore him, until I felt his other hand cupping my cheek. Then I couldn't.

Before I could react, deflect, possibly shove my foot in my mouth further, "Sir, we're at the hospital," came from one of the medics at the front of the vehicle. "We need you to clear out." The back door to the ambulance opened with the other attendant standing there.

"Wait!" I cried out as Dalton began to back out of the rig. "My bag!"

"What is it with you and that bag?" the man grumbled, and then lifted the messenger satchel to show me that it had been with us all along.

"Take it. There are things on the thumb drives that you need to see." The medics proceeded to unload my stretcher from the rig as Dalton stood at my side. "It's about the Wentworth case."

His body stiffened, eyes narrowing on me. "How do you know about that?" he clipped.

I wasn't about to apologize for doing what was right, even if he made me feel like a scolded child just then.

Showing my stubbornness, I jutted my chin up and said, "It doesn't matter. You need to do it right away." I'd be damned if something happened to him, or a member of his team, when I'd been the one to put them in this mess, all thanks to a personal connection.

"Fine. I'll get Brycen to meet me here, then you can show us what you've got when the doctor gives you the all clear."

"No!" Being around him was the last thing I needed. Hell, if working together on that one mission had caused me to lose my head about him, I feared what working with him and his team in person would do. "Just take it. Take the laptops and the thumb drives, too. There's more stuff on those. Brycen will know what to do with it. You won't need me. Just leave me my wallet. It's all I need that's in there."

The man got right in my face, anger, or was it exasperation, emanating from him. It caused me to jerk back into the stretcher's cushions. "You're not getting away from me this time, Devolin," he snapped, his nostrils flaring.

"That's not—"

"You two can do this later," the driver stated. "Miss Taylor, we need to get you back to your room and checked out."

"What?"

Ignoring Dalton's outburst, the medics wheeled me toward the hospital entrance.

CHAPTER 3

DALTON

I was fucking obsessed.

Years ago, I swore I'd never get like this over a woman again and now look at me. Taking that same old stroll down that same old road. Yet, despite how it turned out for me the first time around, here I was, spending the last year using my own company's resources to track down someone who would be deemed, by anyone with a functioning brain, a ghost.

From the moment the mission to rescue Theo's nephew and Morgan ended, White Hat Hussy had disappeared from the deep web, never to be seen or heard from again. Well…sort of.

It was bad enough that her voice has haunted me since *that* night.

The silky, smooth, low and sultry cadence, with a subtle Northern lilt, was never far from my mind. I heard it while out on missions. It was there again when I fell asleep.

Truth be told, I had no idea why, or how for that matter, this woman had infiltrated my thoughts. But random things reminded me of her. I found myself imagining what she looked like. I wondered how old she was, or if she thought of me as often as I did her.

It had been months since I'd seen sign of life from her. A year since I'd last heard her voice. The guys at

Nightshade Securities still gave me hell when I inquired if they'd turned anything up. They thought I'd fallen off my rocker. Maybe I had.

Then again, Devolin made it impossible to forget her.

When my ass landed in the hospital, after being shot, she sent me flowers. I'm not talking about one of those *get-well* bouquets, either. Hell, she'd gone overboard, embarrassing me in front of the others. Even Morgan, a florist for Christ's sake, asked me if I intended on becoming a rival of hers, what with every surface available—and some of the floor—being covered in vase after vase.

But Devolin, our little cyber angel, had gone the extra mile. I hadn't been the only one to suffer her wacky sense of humor, or been blessed with her generosity.

With Shane, she'd help close a bunch of cases that had either gone cold or lacked information to proceed with their current lead. For Morgan and Theo, she'd sent the man a *Mr. T* doll, and a few other more meaningful gifts in celebration of their nuptials. Hell, Brycen might not have thought of it as funny at the time, but the rest of the guys from that night, myself included, thought it was hilarious how she'd infiltrated the computer wiz's system, repeatedly, only to leave dancing babies for him to find. Shit, even Theo's nephew hadn't been left untouched. Jasper had a custom blanket delivered to him, with each one of us guys' names on it. The note it came with, typed up mind you, commended him on his bravery. She also told him that if things ever got scary again, all he had to do was hide under the blanket and that he'd be safe.

Each gift or act had thought put into it. Maybe that's why I was hung up on her, I don't know. Which is why, with every delivery, I pushed the guys to track her down.

But each box or envelope lacked the return address they needed. And forget fingerprints. Each service utilized had no way of providing the billing information, or any information for that matter, because she'd gotten into their systems to erase the data. Items were paid for in cash. The surveillance systems were of no help either. The damn woman had thought of everything to make sure she stayed incognito.

Yet, now I'd found her.

Technically, she found you, dumbass.

And by the looks of things, she wasn't doing very well. So naturally, when a nurse approached me, volunteering to show me to the waiting room, I followed her.

It wasn't until my ass landed in a seat of the Chronic Care Ward, that worry hit me. About the same time it did, so did my stubbornness.

If Devolin thought she could get rid of me, she was mistaken. I'd sit there and wait for as long as it took until I could get to her. I didn't want answers on the Wentworth case from what Brycen could find on her devices. I wanted answers straight from the source. Devolin.